The Crisis of Capitalism
in Inter-War Glasgow:
Five Realist Novels

Sylvia Morgan

humming earth

humming earth
an imprint of
Zeticula Ltd
The Roan
Kilkerran
KA19 8LS
Scotland

http://www.hummingearth.com
admin@hummingearth.com

First published in 2012

ISBN 978-1-84622-033-3

Dedicated with thanks to:

David Keddilty for all his help and support,

and

Irene Maver for the generous sharing of her time and profound knowledge of Glasgow and its history.

Preface

This study examines the economic and social consequences for Glasgow of the global crisis of capitalism known as the Great Depression, and how this is represented in five realist novels published during the 1930s. From a Marxist perspective it is argued that the inter-war era was a time of both cultural renaissance and political revolution, and a liminal moment in Glasgow's history, defining economic and social conditions in the city for most of the twentieth century. It was also a significant phase in the development of the narrative of the city, creating a new form of literary representation of Glasgow, and a new genre of urban realism in Scottish literature.

This book emerged from an M.Phil in Scottish Studies completed in 2010 at the University of Glasgow, supervised by Alan Riach in Scottish Literature and Irene Maver in Scottish History. Having migrated to Scotland in 2001, I discovered a disadvantage encountered by the interloper on another culture is all the required catching up of knowledge assumed by locals who have grown up with it. The advantage can be a sense of anthropological strangeness towards that which is regarded as normal in a society. It has been an arduous apprenticeship, but the struggle with my own ignorance has provided some insight into how the novels examined here, and their historical context, may be presented to other outsiders, as well as those familiar with the culture.

What is unique about this project is the literary review of the five almost forgotten Glasgow novels, together with the historical analysis of the inter-war context within which they were created. This is a considerably contested epoch in the history of Glasgow, a city about which a great deal has been written. The underlying philosophy informing this study is the questioning of a British legacy that values property over humanity. Glasgow has an honourable history of resistance to exploitation driven by the profit motive, a contradiction of continuing relevance given the current global crisis of capitalism. It will soon be a century since these novels were written and much has changed ... but many struggles continue.

Synopsis

The Novels
Hunger March (1934) by Dot Allan
Major Operation (1936) by James Barke
The Shipbuilders (1935) by George Blake
No Mean City (1935) by Alexander McArthur and H. Kingsley Long
Gael Over Glasgow (1937) by Edward Shiels

1 Second City   How was the inter-war era a defining moment of revolution and renaissance in the history of Glasgow, and in the development of the diverse representations of the city?   Do the five realistic novels have value as documentary evidence of life in Glasgow during the inter-war era?

2 City in Crisis What do the novels reveal about the effects of the crisis of capitalism known as the Great Depression during the inter-war era, the reasons for the economic decline of Glasgow as Second City of Empire, and how realistically do they document the subsequent social changes and political consequences when compared with contemporary journalism?

3 City as Protagonist How realistically do the representations and tropes used to signify the city in the novels correspond to contemporary non-fictional depictions of social conditions in Glasgow during the inter-war era?

4 Revolutionary City Did the crisis of capitalism and the phenomenon of Red Clydeside create the necessary and sufficient conditions for a radical political revolution in Glasgow during the inter-war era, and what evidence is there for this in the novels and in contemporary and subsequent political analyses?

5 Consciousness and the City Was false consciousness a major reason for the failure of the ongoing class struggle to evolve nascent revolutionary potential in Glasgow during the inter-war era, and how is this supposition substantiated in the novels?

6 Liminal City Why did the former Second City of Empire, and the novels that represent it so realistically during the inter-war era, slip into a state of permanent liminality?

Abbreviations

The novels are referenced using the following acronyms:

HM —   *Hunger March*
MO —   *Major Operation*
SH —   *The Shipbuilders*
NMC —   *No Mean City*
GG —   *Gael Over Glasgow*

Other acronyms used:

ILP —   Independent Labour Party
BSP —   British Socialist Party
SLP —   Socialist Labour Party
NUWM —   National Unemployed Workers' Movement
NSS —   National Shipbuilders Security Limited
TUC —   Trades Union Congress

Realism, to my mind, implies, besides truth of detail, the truthful reproduction of typical characters under typical circumstances.... The rebellious reaction of the working class against the oppressive medium which surrounds them, their attempts - convulsive, half conscious or conscious - at recovering their status as human beings, belong to history and must therefore lay claim to a place in the domain of realism.

Engels to Margaret Harkness, Marx-Engels Correspondence, 1888

Contents

1   Second City

Context of the novels

The inter-war era between the First and Second World Wars was a major moment of revolution and renaissance for Glasgow, and for the development of representations of the city. During this period Glasgow's identity as the once powerful 'Second City of Empire' began to transform into that of the post-industrial city it was to become in the latter half of the twentieth century. The age was characterised by economic instability created by the shifting demands of the global economy, with the post-war recession of the 1920s developing into the crisis of capitalism known as the Great Depression in the 1930s.[1] Conditions during the inter-war era gave rise to the phenomena of revolutionary Red Clydeside and the Scottish Cultural Renaissance. From this context emerged a new form of literary representation of Glasgow, producing a nascent genre of urban realism in Scottish literature during the 1930s: what became known as 'the realistic proletarian novels of Clydeside'.[2]

Five of these realist novels, defined as 'inter-war' in that they have Glasgow between the two world wars as both their subject matter and date of publication, were identified with the aim of: evaluating their historical significance as documentary evidence of economic, political and social conditions in the city during the inter-war era; and assessing their realism through comparison with non-fictional texts from the period. The five novels are *Hunger March* (1934) by Dot Allan, *Major Operation* (1936) by James Barke, *The Shipbuilders* (1935) by George Blake, *No Mean City* (1935) by Alexander McArthur and H. Kingsley Long, and *Gael Over Glasgow* (1937) by Edward Shiels.[3] All five novels contain realistic representations of the effects

---

1   The global economic recession of the late 2000s is generally acknowledged to be the worst crisis of capitalism since the Great Depression of the 1930s.

2   Sometimes referred to as the novels of 'social realism' – a concept discussed later in this chapter. The term 'social' realism is employed here, rather than 'socialist' realism — now tainted with the negative connotations of the literary doctrine contrived by Stalin, Gorky and Zhdanov for the 1934 Congress of Soviet Writers.

3   The tropes of the titles signify: Glasgow is in need of a major operation to restore its health; the first recorded hunger march in history was that of Jacob's sons to Egypt ('Genesis', *Old Testament*); and 'I am Paul of Tarsus a resident of no mean city' ('Corinthians', *New Testament*).

of the inter-war economic crisis on the city and its people.[4] All are analysed here in terms of their specific historical context, sociological content, and the methods by which they reinforce and reproduce, or subvert and challenge, the dominant class structure of the time. The relationships of power suggested by the texts are deconstructed with reference to the ideologies and institutions; as well as the political, economic, social, and aesthetic concerns of the era. The underlying assumption is that all textual representation either confers agency to, or divests agency from, social groups; and may reveal class struggles and reinforcement of, or revolutionary stances towards, economic forces and social hierarchies in a particular society.

Definitions of 'Glasgow' are subject to ebb and flow, much like the River Clyde at the centre of the city's geographical and historical existence. By the inter-war period, the conurbation around the Clyde was Scotland's largest and most industrialised area; stretching forty miles along the Clyde Valley, from the Firth of Clyde on the West Coast eastwards towards Wishaw in Lanarkshire. The industrial towns were either contiguous or separated only by narrow strips of rural land. During the inter-war era there was the phenomenon of 'Greater Glasgow', created by Glasgow Corporation's absorption of surrounding communities: for example Govan, Partick, and Pollokshaws were separate but adjoining towns until 1912 when, along with other areas, they were incorporated into Glasgow's boundaries, boosting the inhabitants to over one million and making it the most populous city in the United Kingdom after London.[5] Hence the terms 'Glasgow' and 'Clydeside' are used interchangeably here.

The river that runs through Glasgow also runs deep in the collective consciousness of the city — the spatial and temporal character of which has always been intrinsically bound up with the River Clyde.[6] 'The Clyde made Glasgow and Glasgow made the Clyde' is one of the most repeated sayings about the city.[7] The river shaped

---

4   It is only the five novels examined here that fall within this particular narrow definition.

5   Irene Maver. Pers. Comm. University of Glasgow. January 2009.

6   The fate of the river seems inextricably linked with that of the city – it is remarkable how little use Glasgow makes of its river now compared to other great river cities – a malaise possibly indicative of the current lack of confidence of the city – as the city languishes so too does the Clyde?

7   Opening words of 'Seawards the Great Ships', Scotland's first Oscar winning documentary film about the Clyde, and also quoted in numerous other sources.

the shared identity of the Clydeside communities, it underpins the region's history, and it was Glasgow's gateway to the world and shop window for much of its industrial history: so the Clyde functions as a protagonist in its own right, both in the five novels and in reality.[8] In *Glasgow's River* Brian Osborne emphasises this role of the river in the life of the region:

> as a unifying force, as a corridor at the heart of a major region, as a means of communication and as a focus for the identity of the area, its character and culture...The phrase "Clyde Built" has always had an association with quality and with the Clydesiders' pride in the work and life of their river.[9]

Historical Context

The historical narrative of Glasgow has created a range of binary representations of the city in the popular imagination:

Second City or Cancer of Empire
Workshop of the World or the Workers' Republic of Clydeside
Worst slums in Europe or Best Built Suburbs in North Britain
No Mean City or Glasgow's Miles Better
Urban Kailyard or Gangland Glasgow
Dear Green Place or Vomit of a Cataleptic Commercialism
Scottish Renaissance or Scottish Revolution
Semi-Subaltern or Servitor Imperialist
Merchant City or Heartland of Municipal Socialism
Post-Industrial City or Permanently Liminal

The images and stereotypes have shifted, from Glasgow being regarded as one of the 'Second Cities'[10] of the British Empire and economic workshop of the world in the early twentieth century, to the home of mass unemployment and social anomie in the late twentieth century; from Red Clydeside[11] and imminent worker

---

8 Glasgow's 'other rivers' the Kelvin north of the Clyde, and the White Cart south of the Clyde, were intrinsic to the development of Glasgow's early pre-steam industrial revolution, providing a power source for numerous mills along their courses.

9 Brian D.Osborne, and others, *Glasgow's River*, (Lindsay Publications: Glasgow, 1996), p.100.

10 Second City after London — see discussion later in this chapter.

11 See discussion of 'Red Clydeside' in Chapter Four.

revolution during the first three decades of the twentieth century, to 'Glasgow's Miles Better' and 'European City of Culture' in its closing decades. Glasgow is a city internationally famous for the friendliness of its inhabitants, their sense of humour and celebration of language; yet it is also known as the home of poverty, unemployment, religious sectarianism and bad housing. It is a city that recurrently reinvents its own image; yet it may also be enduringly entrapped in the liminal instant of its economic decline. So what is the truth about Glasgow? Like all great iconic cities, the reality is to be found in the complexity of its history rather than the simplicity of its projections. Some of the most enduring stereotypes of the city were created during the inter-war period, a defining time in the economy and culture of Glasgow and in the narrative of the city.

Glasgow was known as the 'Dear Green Place'[12] until the end of the eighteenth century, when the steam power revolution began transforming the city into an industrial metropolis.[13] The resulting radical demographic and structural changes were reflected in the literary and artistic representations from the era. Smoke billowing from factory chimneys and crowded urban landscapes became intrinsic to the imagery of nineteenth century Glasgow. As with many cities in the United Kingdom, the industrial areas of Glasgow were concentrated in the East End of the city, particularly in Calton and Bridgeton, although also in Anderston slightly west of the main business centre, and in the Gorbals and Govan south of the river.[14] These areas were characterised by a radical left wing political tradition,[15] and in turn became the areas most affected and impoverished by the depression of the inter-war economy.[16]

---

12 Glasgow from the Brythonic 'glas cu' or 'glas cau' meaning more prosaically 'green hollow' but romantically translated into 'dear green place'. Glasgow was described by Daniel Defoe in *A Tour through England and Wales*, 1707 as: 'the cleanest and beautifullest, and best built city in Britain, London excepted'.

13 1800 was the year the patent expired on James Watt's steam engine opening it to the market.

14 The prevailing winds in the UK are from the west carrying the air pollution eastwards, so industrial areas and working class residential areas are usually to the east of cities, and bourgeois residential areas are to the west, as in Glasgow and London.

15 Documented by David Kirkwood, *My Life of Revolt*, (Harrap & Co: London, 1935) pp.1-10

16 For a full discussion of the economic history of modern Glasgow see Anthony Slaven, *The Development of the West of Scotland*, 1750-1960, (Routledge & Kegan Paul: London, 1975)

Marketed in the late twentieth century as Europe's first post-industrial city; Glasgow had also been one of Europe's first great industrial cities — an identity that had developed from the late eighteenth century onwards. The city was perfectly placed in terms of the conditions conducive to early capitalist development: proximity to the natural resources of coal and iron required for heavy industry; an earlier accumulation of mercantile capital from tobacco, sugar and textile trade with the colonies; and unlimited supplies of cheap labour necessary for the accrual of surplus value. This army of labour was made possible by the economic forces both pushing the traditional peasantry off the land, famine and land dispossession known as the 'Clearances' in the Scottish Lowlands and Highlands, and in Ireland; and pulling the nascent urban proletariat towards the cities in the hope of subsistence in a wage economy, subsequently developed, in the engineering and shipbuilding workshops of Clydeside, into one of the most highly skilled industrial workforces in the world.

Glasgow's success as a shipbuilding city was made possible by an earlier phase of industrialisation in the eighteenth century, originally based in textile manufacture, which then evolved into a second more sustained phase of heavy industry, and subsequently into the development of shipbuilding along the Clyde from the 1830s. From the late 1820s new technology, along with the abundance of iron and coal in the Lanarkshire area adjoining Glasgow, promoted iron production; and later steel production from the late 1870s. From this time until the inter-war era, the journalistic tropes used to describe Glasgow's mining and heavy industry emphasised strength and reliability and a particular pride in 'Clyde-built'. For example Robert Gillespie wrote in 1876:

> neither the Clyde nor Glasgow would be what they now are were it not for the vast mineral fields which lie north and south of the river, and which yield such ample and unfailing supplies of the backbone of civilisation – iron, and of coal the material from which is drawn the nervous power to vivify that backbone.[17]

An important contribution to the promotion of Glasgow's shipbuilding industry in the nineteenth century was the ongoing project, enhanced by Victorian engineering, of widening and deepening the Clyde; not a navigable river for large vessels in its

---

17 Robert Gillespie, *Glasgow and The Clyde*, (Robert Forrester: Glasgow, 1876) p. 25

natural state. Irene Maver argues that the imagery of the Clyde's expansion was most important for perceptions of Glasgow's industrial development — the idea of the channelling of the river for commerce and the common good.[18] By the 1870s the Clyde was being hailed as the great generator of Glasgow's prosperity, a linkage emphasised at the time by Gillespie:

> What the Nile was to Egypt, the Clyde is to Glasgow. It is the source in a large measure of that prosperity which has raised, in recent years, a town once of comparatively minor importance to the lofty position of "Second city in the Empire".[19]

There was of course a great deal more to Glasgow's economy than shipbuilding. But Glasgow was identified, and identified itself, as a significant shipbuilding city, and the skill and expertise involved in the production of great ocean-going vessels became an emblem of pride and power for the city and its workers. The prestige value of the shipbuilding industry and the awareness of this in the city and its inhabitants at the start of the twentieth century is emphasised by James Hamilton Muir in 1901:

> We believe, every Glasgow man of us, that our shipbuilding is a thing to be talked of, and a most honourable and dignified business to have for the chief industry of a city. Sheffield is known to the world for cutlery, Birmingham for pedlars' wares and nails and bullets, and Manchester for "Manchester goods." But Glasgow is the maker of ships, and her sons are proud of their seemly product ... of more moment to Glasgow than her other industries, her college, her cathedral, is the building of her ships.[20]

The buoyant imagery and eulogistic references to the Clyde and to Glasgow's status as proud shipbuilding city and 'Second City' in these earlier descriptions is in contradistinction to the downswing in popular portrayals of the city during the inter-war period, particularly those of the 'Condition of Scotland' discourse (discussed later in this chapter). The economic powerhouse that had been Glasgow throughout the nineteenth century subsequently

---

18 Irene Maver, *Glasgow* (Edinburgh University Press: Edinburgh, 2000), pp, 45-46 and 122-23.

19 Gillespie, *Glasgow and The Clyde*, p.24

20 James Hamilton Muir, *Glasgow in 1901* (William Hodge & Co: Edinburgh, 1901), pp. 116-18.

became one of the areas in Britain worst affected by the global economic depressions of the early twentieth century. Owing to a peculiar confluence of historical causalities, Glasgow began to face an economic slump from 1921 with devastating effects on its heavy industry and shipbuilding-based economy. The complex reasons, if not the remedies, for the periodic crises that occur within capitalism are perhaps better, if still imperfectly, understood now than they were in the inter-war era. From interpretations of the situation that arose during the inter-war era it is possible to distil three main contemporary justifications for the economic decline in Scotland: failure of initiative from Scottish entrepreneurs to adapt to changes in technology and the global economy; failure of Scotland to attract investment due to its remoteness from major centres; and failure of the militant unionised workforce to understand that the cost of labour had increased beyond the profit incentive in the labour-intensive industries upon which the Glasgow economy was based.[21] There are ironic inconsistencies inherent in all three explanations, as it had been the initiative and innovation of Glasgow's entrepreneurs and the industry and skill of its workforce that had played a large part in the development, not only of Glasgow, but also of the entire United Kingdom during the Industrial Revolution, and this despite the region's remote geographic placement. In fact, Glasgow's position on the west coast of Scotland had been extremely favourable to its role in the development of the Atlantic trade with British colonies, and the River Clyde was the global gateway for this purpose. (The economics of the inter-war era are discussed in Chapter Two.)

The economic problems of the inter-war years were exacerbated by the complex political dynamics of the region: the reputation of Clydeside for difficult industrial relations; job demarcation and protectionism by the trades unions; the emphasis of the owners of the means of production on short term profit rather than long term planning; and an economic policy determined by the centralised Westminster government far from the economic realities of Scotland. During the Great Depression, in a futile attempt at economic rationalisation, government policy for regeneration was geared towards reduction in costs, resulting in wage cuts and

---

21 From economic analyses of the inter-war era – see discussion of the 'Condition of Scotland' discourse later in this chapter.

worker redundancy.[22] The consequent massive unemployment, increasing immiseration, and growing militancy of the working class, contributed to the development of Glasgow's reputation as a revolutionary city. The mining, metal-working and shipbuilding industries had nurtured a tradition of radical politics in Glasgow and its surrounding areas. It was this context which was to create many of the Red Clydesiders and produce the perceived potential for revolution in Glasgow during the inter-war era. (The politics of the inter-war era are discussed in Chapter Four.)

Historically, Victorian Glasgow politics had been dominated by free-trade Liberalism – representing class cohesion not class conflict. Liberal politics then became marginalised when class politics came to the fore during the 1920s.[23] But even before that, the internal problems in the Liberal Party encouraged the emergence of what Iain Hutchison, in his analysis of the growth of socialism in Glasgow, refers to as 'a new socialist strand ... appealing to the working classes of the city'.[24] The Scottish Labour Party was formed in 1888, and five years later joined the British-wide Independent Labour Party (ILP).[25] Until 1914 the ILP was 'easily the largest socialist organisation in Glasgow' according to Hutchison, with branches in most districts of the city.[26] Many of the well known Clydeside inter-war politicians emerged from an ILP background of 'municipal socialist' politics in the Glasgow Corporation. In the first two decades of the twentieth century, housing was a big campaign issue for the ILP. The Clydeside Rent Strikes of 1915 shifted the balance of power against the private landlords and in favour of municipal housing; entrenched problems with housing continued during the inter-war period, and the need to solve the 'slum question' was a concern that came to have iconic status for Glasgow socialists.[27] (Social issues of the inter-war era are discussed in Chapter Three.)

22 Similar to the historically ignorant and short-sighted measures introduced by the UK Tory/LibDem Government in 2010, resulting in increased popular political resistance.

23 Maver, *Glasgow,* p.120.

24 Iain Hutchison, 'Glasgow working class politics' in R.A. Cage (ed.), *The Working Class in Glasgow, 1750-1914* (Croom Helm: London, 1987), pp.98-141.)

25 The rise of the Labour Party in Glasgow is documented in J. J. Smyth, *Labour in Glasgow, 1896-1936: Socialism, Suffrage, Sectarianism* (Tuckwell Press: East Linton, 2000); and Alan McKinlay and R. J. Morris (eds), *The ILP on Clydeside, 1893-1932: from Foundation to Disintegration* (Manchester University Press: Manchester, 1991).

26 Hutchison, *The Working Class in Glasgow, 1750-1914*, p.115

27 Maver, *Glasgow*, pp.258-260

The inter-war years were a liminal moment of becoming for Scotland, when the old was not yet terminated and the new was struggling to emerge. Liminality refers to a state of cultural transition, during which normal limits to thought and boundaries of behaviour shift, opening the way to nascent possibilities of social being. However this state can become permanent when the transition is not fully completed. It is argued here that during the inter-war years Glasgow was caught in a liminal historical moment, one of shifting world trade patterns when the global economic order was being redefined. It was a time of twentieth-century technological modernisation, to which the nineteenth-century based Glasgow industries did not adjust well. Ongoing failure of economic vision and adaptation led to the city being caught in a state of permanent liminality from which it could be argued it has never successfully moved forward. It was during the inter-war period that Glasgow, the once powerful industrial, self-proclaimed Second City of Empire, began to evolve its post-modern, post-industrial identity. (The socio-economic legacy of the inter-war era is discussed in Chapter Six.)

The 'Second City' label continued to underpin Glasgow's rather shaky self-image as an imperial city during the inter-war years. However 'Second City' status was always contested territory, with similar claims made by other great British industrial cities such as Liverpool and Manchester: from the nineteenth century Edinburgh and Dublin rivalled each other for the title. Although Glasgow had over a million inhabitants by 1938[28] it was no longer the Second City in population terms,[29] as in the wider context of the British Empire there were cities of much greater population size than Glasgow.[30] After the First World War the heavy-industry based economy of the city became increasingly marginalised due to changing global economics. It briefly revived during the rearmament of the Second World War, hung on for a while in the following decades, and then eventually entered its death throes in the 1960s. While it has succeeded in reinventing certain aspects of itself, Glasgow never recovered its former glory and wealth. The five realistic proletarian

---

28 The population of 1938 was almost double that of Glasgow in 2009.
29 Maver, *Glasgow*, p.208.
30 W. Hamish Fraser, 'Competing with the Capital: The Case of Glasgow Versus Edinburgh', in Lars Nilsson (ed) *Capital Cities: Images and realities in the Historical Development of European Capital Cities*, (Institute of Urban History: Stockholm University, 2000).

novels of the inter-war era are examined here as evidence of the social and historical changes in Glasgow in the early stages of its transformation process from industrial to post-industrial city.

Scottish Renaissance or Revolution?

By the inter-war years the Clyde industrial region had the image of being the 'Workshop of the World', the 'Engine Room of Britain' and, particularly after the First World War, the 'Arsenal of the Empire'. Nevertheless, the shipbuilders, the miners, the engineers, and the factory workers who created the profits that made this public relations hyperbole possible, were paid poverty wages and forced to live in overcrowded squalor. Vast wealth was generated in all areas of Glasgow's industries, but those who actually produced it shared little. This was the context from which an increasingly militant worker organisation emerged on Clydeside during the first decades of the twentieth century.

The extraordinarily difficult conditions endured by the proletariat during the development of the city had produced a distinctively Glaswegian culture, the complexities of which Seán Damer deconstructs: 'Glaswegians acted creatively on their grossly unfavourable working and living conditions to construct a culture which is uniquely tough, resilient, warm and witty'.[31] It was a working class organic intellectual culture, but one which also became appropriated and represented by middle class cultural practitioners. The phenomenon known as the Scottish Renaissance emerged in the early 1920s and evolved until the Second World War in 1939.[32] According to Alan Riach it was Hugh MacDiarmid who heralded this Scottish Renaissance as: 'an activation of national cultural awareness...an attempt to demolish the weight of convention suffocating creativity'.[33] The objective of those involved in the Scottish Renaissance was a re-evaluation of Scottish culture, a realistic reappraisal of the socio-economic condition of Scotland, and

---

31 Seán Damer, (1990), *Glasgow Going for a Song*, (Lawrence & Wishart Ltd: London) p.102.

32 The Scottish Renaissance was the cultural response, in the form of a literary movement, to the social and economic crisis of capitalism in Scotland between the wars. The political response was the Scottish National Party founded in 1926.

33 Alan Riach, *Representing Scotland in Literature, Popular Culture and Iconography: The Masks of the Modern Nation* (Palgrave MacMillan: Basingstoke, 2005), p.xxi.

a challenge to previously distorted representations of the nation.[34] The project was to create a coherent, dynamic, artistic revival, integrated with a regeneration of the social, economic, and political life of Scotland, and developed across the spectrum of cultural producers: writers in Scottish fiction and non-fiction, journalists, intellectuals, artists, and politicians.

An intrinsic element of the Scottish Renaissance was the 'Condition of Scotland' discourse published during the inter-war era, offering a non-fictional analysis of the prevailing problems in the nation. Examples of this discourse are: James A. Bowie, *The Future of Scotland* (1939);[35] John Boyd Orr, 'Scotland as it is' (1937) and 'Scotland as it might be' (1937);[36] Andrew Dewar Gibb, *Scotland in Eclipse* (1930);[37] Alexander Maclehose, *The Scotland of Our Sons* (1937);[38] William Power, *Scotland and the Scots* (1934);[39] George Malcolm Thomson, *Caledonia or the Future of the Scots* (1927)[40] and *Scotland: That Distressed Area* (1935).[41] Moreover there were writers, whose main focus was more usually the production of fiction, who added their voices to the 'Condition of Scotland' debates. For example: George Blake, *The Heart of Scotland* (1934);[42] Lewis Grassic Gibbon and Hugh MacDiarmid, *Scottish Scene* (1934);[43] Edwin Muir, *Scottish Journey* (1935);[44] and Edward Scouller, 'So this is Glasgow!' (1936).[45]

The 'Condition of Scotland' writers engaged in diverse forms of literary expression: autobiographical, travel-writing, life-writing,

34 William Power, *My Scotland* (Porpoise Press: Edinburgh, 1934), p.300.
35 James A. Bowie, *The Future of Scotland: A Survey of the Present Position with Some Prospects of Future Policy* (W&R Chambers: Edinburgh, 1939).
36 John Boyd Orr, 'Scotland as it is' and 'Scotland as it might be', in *The Scotland of our Sons,* (ed) A Maclehose (Alexander Maclehose:London: 1937), p.64 -83 and p.84 -109.
37 Andrew Dewar Gibb, *Scotland in Eclipse* (Humphrey Toulmin: London,1930).
38 Alexander Maclehose, in *The Scotland of Our Sons* (ed) A Maclehose (Alexander Maclehose:London:1937).
39 William Power, *Scotland and the Scots* (Moray Press: Edinburgh, 1934).
40 George Malcolm Thomson, *Caledonia or the Future of the Scots* (Kegan Paul: London, 1927).
41 George Malcolm Thomson, *Scotland: That Distressed Area* (Porpoise Press: Edinburgh: 1935).
42 George Blake, *The Heart of Scotland* (Batcsford: London1934).
43 Lewis Grassic Gibbon, 'Glasgow', in *Scottish Scene* and *A Scots Hairst,* (Hutchinson: London, 1967, repr.1978)
44 Edwin Muir, *Scottish Journey* (Mainstream Publishing: Edinburgh: 1935:1979).
45 Edward Scouller, 'So this is Glasgow!' *Outlook*, vol.1, no 8, November (1936), pp.79-81.

and journalism. This continues to be an under-researched area, one in which Margery McCulloch is one of the few documenters. In *Modernism and Nationalism: Literature and Society in Scotland 1918 –1939* (2004) McCulloch has collated primary source documents from the inter-war era, with the stated aim of bringing to the reading public the debates and arguments: 'concerning the wider cultural, social and political forces at work at home and abroad during this challenging transitional period.' Pertinent to an analysis of the five realist inter-war novels is McCulloch's suggestion that, 'It may also be the case that a more acute understanding of the creative writing and writers of the period will be arrived at as a result of their work being seen in the context of such contemporaneous material'.[46]

A popular theme of the 'Condition of Scotland' debates concerned 'What's wrong with Scotland'. The pervasive image of Scotland was that of a 'distressed area', to be unfavourably compared with the more prosperous England. In an article entitled 'Scotland as it is', John Boyd Orr highlighted the historical irony of the Scots' major contribution to the building of the British Empire, in relation to their poor share in its prosperity compared to the better-off English. In fact Boyd Orr argued, 'the whole of Scotland might well be scheduled as a distressed area'.[47] Furthermore, in the aptly entitled: *Scotland, That Distressed Area*, the Scottish Nationalist journalist George Malcolm Thomson posited that, far from experiencing economic progress after the 1707 Union with England, for Scotland, 'the hands of the clock had begun to move backwards'.[48] McCulloch avers that Thomson's texts provided 'wide-ranging and influential analyses of decline in Scotland',[49] (unfortunately however, both Thomson and Andrew Dewar Gibb's credibility were undermined by their sectarian attacks on Irish immigration and the Catholic Church).[50]

The 'what's wrong with Scotland?' debate came to be deeply ingrained in the contemporary discourse around Scotland's economic difficulties after the First World War.[51]   Edmund

---

46 Margery Palmer McCulloch,(ed.) *Modernism and Nationalism: Literature and Society in Scotland 1918 – 1939 Source documents for the Scottish Renaissance* (The Association for Scottish Literary Studies University of Glasgow: Glasgow, 2004), p.xiii.

47 Boyd Orr, 'Scotland as it is', p.64.

48 Thomson, *Scotland: That Distressed Area*, p.5.

49 McCulloch, (ed.) *Modernism and Nationalism*, p.385.

50 Maver, Pers. Comm. University of Glasgow. July 2009.

51 Richard, J. Finlay, 'National Identity in Crisis: Politicians, Intellectuals and the

Stegmaier's discussion of these texts (although he does not refer to them as 'Condition of Scotland') posits that they were grounded in a 'particularly Scottish analysis' of the nation's problems, with an emphasis on factual accounts, based on statistical data, and offering an alternative vision of the future.[52] This debate was also influenced by an underlying fear of social disintegration in the inter-war zeitgeist, an anxiety exploited by Glasgow's large and influential popular press. Maver argues that, 'The deteriorating urban fabric was used as a metaphor for Scotland's declining industrial prosperity. Assorted writers exploited the image of negativity to strengthen their case for remedial action'.[53] Nostalgia for pre-war success contributed to the media constructions of the post First World War city as sinister, creating the insidious image of Glasgow as the 'Cancer of Empire'.[54] This in itself worked as a self-fulfilling, self-perpetuating prophecy.

This negative tendency in the discourse is in contradistinction to a more positive development, described by William Power in *Scotland and the Scots* (1934) as 'the new travel writing' of the inter-war period, an attempt by Scottish writers to escape the confines of the industrialised cities and the urban misery of the Depression.[55] Power wrote: 'The whole of Scottish literature of today, indeed, including the majority of books by Scots about Scotland, represents mainly the discovery of Scotland by the Scots'.[56] This sentiment is evident in *Gael Over Glasgow*, *Major Operation*, and *The Shipbuilders*, and became an expression of Scottish Nationalist politics in the 1930s. The later 'Scotland on the Move' discourse, embodied in the realistic films of John Grierson, builds upon this more positive trend.[57] The role of the press and journalists was consistent and important in shaping the imagery of Glasgow and is discussed more thoroughly in Chapters Three and Four, particularly in relation to the concepts of Gangland Glasgow and Red Clydeside.

"End of Scotland" 1920-1939. *History*, 79 (1994), pp. 242-259

52 Edmund Stegmaier, 'Facts and Vision in Scottish Writing of the 1920s and 1930s'. *Scottish Literary Journal*, 9, Nov 1982, pp.67-78.
53 Maver, *Glasgow* ,p.253.
54 Maver, Ibid. ,p.234.
55 The discovery of Scotland by the Scots as opposed to the discovery of Scotland by the English, first with Dr Johnson then the landscape painters such as Knox.
56 Power, *Scotland and the Scots*, p.30.
57 John Grierson, (1979), 'The Salt of the Earth' in Forsyth Hardy (ed), *John Grierson's Scotland*, (Ramsay Head Press: Edinburgh, 1979)

The possibilities of individual agency versus economic determinism experienced by the characters in the inter-war novels are discussed in Chapter Five. This chapter also examines the power of ideology, and whether false consciousness was a reason for the failure of the ongoing class struggle to evolve its nascent revolutionary potential in Glasgow during the inter-war era. The analysis here is grounded in the Marxist concept that from the economic base or infrastructure of society emerges a superstructure consisting of definite forms of social consciousness. Politics, religion, aesthetics, and ethics are all instruments of ideology which Marxist theory attempts to deconstruct.

However Marx and Engels did not produce a comprehensive theory of ideology or culture. Terry Eagleton, building on the work of Raymond Williams, discusses this issue at some length, arguing that a Marxist theory of culture will emphasise complexity, diversity and contradictions. Eagleton reminds us that, 'ideological is not synonymous with cultural: it denotes, more precisely, the points at which our cultural practices are interwoven with political power.'[58] Williams elaborates on the idea of the superstructure as a matter of human consciousness that includes continuities from the past as well as reactions to the present, 'Marx indeed at times regards ideology as a false consciousness:[59] a system of continuities which change has in fact undermined'.[60] Detailed information about how people felt and thought at a particular time, is often only available to us in literature, therefore 'To understand literature, then, means understanding the total social process of which it is a part.'[61] Engels, and later Lenin, believed that realistic novels can tell us more about the nature of society than can sociological, political and historical analysis. However Williams avers that much 'English' Marxist criticism 'seems to subscribe simultaneously to a mechanistic view of art as the passive 'reflex' of the economic base, and to a Romantic belief in art as projecting an ideal world and stirring men to new values'.[62] Eagleton argues for the dialectical complexity of ideology which 'is never a simple reflection of a ruling class's ideas; on the contrary, it is

---

61 Terry Eagleton, *Marxism and Literary Criticism,* (London: Methuen, 1976), p.5
59 Although Engels used the actual term 'false consciousness', Marx did not.
60 Raymond Williams, *Culture and Society.* (Hogarth: London, 1958 repr.1982) p.266
61 Eagleton, *Marxism and Literary Criticism*, p.5
62 Williams, *Culture and Society.* p.273

always a complex phenomenon, which may incorporate conflicting, even contradictory views of the world.'[63] These are contradictions that materialize within the narratives of the inter-war novels, the characters within the novels, and may reflect those of the writers themselves. (The relevance of these concepts to an analysis of the inter-war Glasgow novels is discussed in Chapter Six.)

The Realistic Novels of Clydeside

A new genre of urban novels developed in Scottish literature during the inter-war years. Authored in Glasgow and therefore 'Clydebuilt', these became known as the proletarian or realistic novels of Clydeside. Five of these novels, with inter-war Glasgow as both their subject and period of publication, have been traced and examined here for their realistic representation of the city and its people. The defining feature of these realist novels is that all contain some reference to the social and economic effects of the Great Depression, and to the alienation and anomie produced by the reification inherent in capitalist social relations. From the perspective of seven decades after their creation, it is possible to assess the veracity of the novels as historical documents by comparison with the evidence of contemporaneous non-fictional representations of Glasgow; particularly the 'Condition of Scotland' debates.

An enigma for critics of Scottish literature is that up until the inter-war years, there was a dearth of realistic representation of the city in the form of an urban industrial novel genre. In the 1980s Moira Burgess presented a critical re-evaluation of the Glasgow novel,[64] in which she argues that the Glasgow novels of the inter-war era portrayed the city in fiction for the first time in all its gritty reality. Roderick Watson posits that late Victorians did not want to read about their industrial and urban realities and so: 'Scottish Fiction ended the century with a vision of itself which was parochial, sentimental and almost entirely given over to nostalgia'.[65] Burgess refers to 'a strange blind spot in Scottish fiction, the ignoring by most novelists of the urban and industrial scene in favour of the rural and parochial'. She suggests three possible reasons for this:

---

63 Eagleton, *Marxism and Literary Criticism,* p.7
64 Burgess is the acknowledged historian of the Glasgow novel.
65 Moira Burgess, *The Glasgow Novel 3rd Edition* (The Scottish Library Association: Glasgow, 1999) pp.313-314

the exceptionally swift and brutal impact of the Industrial Revolution, with, as it were, a stupefying effect on contemporary writers; the influence of Scott's novels with their historical-romantic view of Scotland; and a desire to record, with perhaps more enthusiasm than accuracy, the picturesque elements of an obsolescent way of life. [66]

In 1934, around the time of the emergence of the new realistic genre in the Glasgow novel, Power commented on its favourable contradistinction to the previously dominant style in Scotland of the so-called 'Kailyard': 'The average Scottish writer no longer views his own country through the narrow and distorting media of feudal romanticism, Kailyard sentimentalism, or Imperialist insularity'.[67] Watson traces the origin of the term Kailyard to 1894,[68] arguing that 'the case of the Kailyard reveals much about the complicated nature of Scottish cultural identity':

> the Kailyard is against change, and when it looks to the past – usually one generation back – it describes a timeless stasis of isolated rural communities whose dramas revolve around the doings of the minister of the dominie – arrivals, departures, weddings, funerals and the pitfalls of petty presumption. It must be admitted that these themes belong within the Scottish tradition of feeling and domestic realism, but is has sadly dwindled to a sentimental subgenre. [69]

Edwin Muir likewise saw the popularity of the Kailyard literary tradition in industrialised Scotland as a harkening back to a romanticised rural past, a comfort and refuge from a brutalised urban present, and a product of the nation's religious and economic history:

> Two things mainly contributed to set Scotland, an eminently realistic country, on such a path: the breakdown of Calvinism, a process salutary in itself, but throwing off as a by-product an obliterating debris of sentimentality, and the rise of an industrial system so sordid and disfiguring that people were eager to escape from it by any road, however strange. [70]

---

66 Ibid. pp. 31-32.
67 Power, *Scotland and the Scots*, p.30.
68 J.H. Millar in *New Review* (1894) attacked a collection of tales published by Ian Maclaren as 'cabbage-patch – kailyard – writing'
69 Roderick Watson, *The Literature of Scotland.* (MacMillan: London, 1984) pp.314-315
70 Muir, *Scottish Journey,* pp. 67-68

In *Barrie and the Kailyard School* (1951) George Blake, the Glasgow journalist and one of the novelists examined here, was similarly critical of the sentimentalising escapist Kailyard genre because, as he argues in a later text *The Annals of Scotland (1956)*, it was incapable of portraying the true miserable reality of industrialised Scotland: 'So we ask what the contemporary Scottish writers had to say about this almost melodramatic state of affairs ... Was there nobody in Scotland to tell the truth about what was happening?'[71] Burgess defines Kailyard as: 'a body of work characterised by sentimentality, narrowness of vision, and the acceptance of a code of unshakeable assumptions regarding conventional conduct and belief'.[72] Kailyard was a term usually applied to fiction with a rural setting, and in order to describe city fiction with these qualities, Burgess claims to have invented the term 'Urban Kailyard'.[73]

In tracing the development of the realistic Glasgow urban novel Burgess divides the inter-war period into the 1920s and 1930s. She argues that initial attempts at urban realism in the 1920s 'have not survived to the present day in either popular favour or critical esteem', but that they laid the groundwork and provided 'a first draft of the realistic Glasgow novel'.[74] However she believes that the novels of the 1930s were a different phenomenon in that they evinced 'a new political and social commitment'.[75] Unfortunately these very 1930s Glasgow novels that Burgess regards as a development in the realistic genre have also not survived in popular favour with the reading public, with the possible exception of *No Mean City*,[76] and there is little evidence of their receiving much critical esteem. It can be argued that all succeed more on a level of social commentary than on their literary merit, and ironically it was *No Mean City* and *The Shipbuilders*, the two novels out of the five that could best be described as fitting the term 'Urban Kailyard', that became iconic representations of Glasgow within the popular consciousness. Burgess herself articulates reservations about the merit of some of the 1930s novels and regards *No Mean City* as being a particularly

71 George Blake, *The Annals of Scotland 1895-1955* (BBC: London,1956) p.10-11.
72 Moira Burgess, *Imagine a City: Glasgow in Fiction* (Argyll Publishing: Glendaruel, 1998), p.68.
73 Burgess, *Imagine a City: Glasgow in Fiction*. p.69.
74 Moira Burgess, *The Glasgow Novel, 3rd ed.* p.45.
75 Ibid.
76 Ibid.

negative influence on the genre.[77] However in the second edition of her critical text *The Glasgow Novel* (1986), she selects three of these novels as being of major significance for the decade: *The Shipbuilders* (1935), *Major Operation* (1936), and *Gael Over Glasgow* (1937). In the third edition of her text she adds a fourth significant novel to her list, *Hunger March*(1934). *No Mean City* has been included in this analysis for the reason that it shares the thematic emphasis of the other four inter-war proletarian novels: the effects of the Depression and unemployment on Glasgow and its inhabitants.

For the most part, the five novels discussed here present a picture of Glasgow which can be regarded as 'realistic'. Realism in literature is an approach that attempts to describe life without idealisation or romantic subjectivity and concerns itself with social settings and the nature of society. Insofar as the primary focus of the inter-war novels discussed here is upon the working classes and social structures, and because of the social and political commitment of the novels (albeit to varying degrees), it could be argued that they belong to the genre of 'social realism'[78]. This literature is grounded in Marxist theory and presupposes that perceptions of reality derive from class-consciousness. The aesthetic of Georges Lukács, the Marxist cultural theorist, is based on the premise that *all* literature is a reflection of reality, and that it will be the truest mirror if it fully reflects the contradictions of social development. There is also an ethical implication in that social realism should demonstrate insight into the class structure of society and the future direction of its evolution.[79] Eagleton argues that for Lukács, 'all great art is socially progressive in the sense that, whatever the author's conscious political allegiance', that which is created will realise and reflect the 'vital world-historical forces of an epoch which make for change and growth ...the great realist writers arise from a history which is visibly in the making'.[80] It is argued in Chapter Four that the inter-war era in Glasgow was just such a turbulent potential revolutionary epoch of change, the significance of which the writers of the realist novels were aware and attempting to represent. Realism

77 Burgess,*Ibid*, p.40.
78 The term 'social' realism is employed here, rather than 'socialist' realism — now tainted with the negative connotations of the literary doctrine contrived by Stalin, Gorky and Zhdanov for the 1934 Congress of Soviet Writers.
79 Georges Lukács, The Meaning of Contemporary Realism, (Merlin Press: London, 1963) p.7 & p.48.
80 Eagleton, *Marxism and Literary Criticism*, p.29

for Lukács is a genuinely dialectical art form which mediates and reconciles the capitalist contradictions between abstract and concrete, essence and appearance, the individual and the social whole. Realism mirrors the complex totality of society itself, and in so doing it combats the alienation and fragmentation of capitalist society, projecting a complex possibility of human wholeness and harmony.[81] The implications of these ideas are discussed in Chapter Six in relation to the interpretation of the inter-war novels, their inherent contradictions, and their nostalgia and related inability to articulate an alternative progressive vision of the future.

Of all the novels examined here, the one most befitting of the label 'social realism' is *Major Operation*. The novel narrates descriptions of the economic decline of Glasgow during the inter-war years and the response of the workers to the inter-war crisis of capitalism, in a manner corresponding more successfully with reality than the other novels. *Major Operation* recounts the historic events of the United Kingdom hunger marches of the 1930s with more detailed realism than that of the novel entitled *Hunger March,* which takes as its subject a twenty four hour period in Glasgow covering one such march. *Major Operation* also dissects the devastating effects of unemployment on the working class more realistically than *The Shipbuilders*, which takes as its main theme the demise of the shipbuilding industry. *Major Operation* also contains a more radical historical materialist analysis of the social unrest that affected Clydeside than *Gael Over Glasgow,* the novel which takes this subject as its main theme; although *Major Operation* cannot surpass this last novel for realistic descriptions of the working life of the area during the inter-war era. Furthermore the exposure of the degradation of the slums in *Major Operation* is as realistic as, but less melodramatic than, that of *No Mean City* which takes this theme as its main concern.

It has been argued that *No Mean City* veers too far into naturalism to be classified as 'social realism'. According to Lukács, naturalism in writing is concerned only with the surface appearances of everyday life, deprived of the historical conditions of its existence and so drained of direction and meaning.[82] Jack Mitchell posits that with *No Mean City*, proletarian social realism in Scotland, 'allowed naturalism to get in first and queer the pitch ... showing the proletarian community teeming with dynamic life, with its own morality and specific

81 Lukács, *The Meaning of Contemporary Realism,* p.76
82 Ibid. p.33.

human relations — all twisted into their opposites'.[83] He is almost as condemnatory of *The Shipbuilders*, positing the possibility that *Major Operation* was consciously intended to work against these two novels, intimating that a literary antidote to their negative influence was needed. However C.P. Snow argues against the oversimplified definitions of novels as 'realist', 'naturalist', 'symbolist', into which most do not fit neatly: 'In particular the distinction between realism and naturalism has been argued about inconclusively for a hundred years.' [84]

It can be posited that *No Mean City* reflects the effects of the Depression on the lives of the working class with adequate realism, and is therefore a useful portrait of the city during the inter-war era. It contains descriptions of the economic working day of the industrial city other than shipbuilding and heavy industry, and is notable for detailing the minutiae of domestic life, housing, and courting rituals; as well as unemployment, gang violence, and criminality on the margins of the economy.

The central narrative structure of four of the novels (other than *No Mean City*) presents the parallel lives of representative members of the proletariat and the bourgeoisie; the parallel plots comparing the ways in which the economic crises of the inter-war years shape these characters, and the similar and differing life and work experiences of these two classes in Glasgow. In *The Shipbuilders* the two class representatives are Danny Shields the shipyard riveter, and his previous army comrade and current employer shipyard owner Leslie Pagan. *Major Operation* concerns the bringing together in the same hospital ward of Jock MacKelvie a shipyard worker, and George Anderson a bourgeois business man, simultaneously in hospital to have an emergency 'major operation'. In *Gael Over Glasgow* the parallel plot device is similar though not as straightforward as in the other novels, Brian O'Neill a working class trainee shipyard engineer meets his middle class counterpart Alec Cameron, when they are both roaming the hills above Clydebank. In *Hunger March* the bourgeois life of Arthur Joyce the owner of 'Joyce's India Merchants', is set up in opposition to that of his cleaner, working class Mrs Humphry and her unemployed son Joe. The fifth novel *No Mean City* differs somewhat

83 Jack Mitchell 'The struggle for the working class novel in Scotland'. *Scottish Marxist*. Part III no 8 January (1975), p.39.
84 C.P. Snow, *The Realists: Portraits of Eight Novelists* (MacMillan: London, 1978) p.8.

from the other four in theme and structure. Although also concerned with class difference, the main class opposition is between the working class anti-hero gangster Johnnie Stark and Glasgow itself. He is the faecal figure, a by-product of the industrial digestion of the Second City, and an integral aspect of the dark side of its capitalist identity.

The five realist novels all take as their subject matter the economic crisis of capitalism in Glasgow during the inter-war years and its socio-political consequences. All illustrate the long term effect of economic deprivation on the Glasgow working class. All share the themes of: unemployment, the dole, class struggle, class consciousness, the possibility of impending revolution and the deterrents to revolution — notably false consciousness and alcohol. All contain an overt critique of the capitalist system, together with the writers' commitment to presenting it realistically. All contain a condemnation of the ills of urbanisation and express a loss of innocence caused by the corrupting city.

But the realistic inter-war novels also express a celebration of the complexity and energy of Glasgow, and serve as a testament to the life of the city at a particularly important moment in its development. So a range of themes are apparent within the designation of liminal city; the impact of the First World War being one of the most crucial as the Red Clydeside image arose directly from that conflict.

Together with these shared themes discussed above, each novel contains its own specific thematic emphasis. Some of the novels document for posterity the working life of the Clyde shipbuilding industry and the social life of its skilled communities, and some of them emphasise politics and the labour movement; demonstrations and hunger marches. *Hunger March* recounts the decline of business in Glasgow, and the political demonstrations during the economic crisis. *Gael Over Glasgow* details the practical working life, the factories and shipbuilding yards, and the trade union politics of Clydeside. *The Shipbuilders* records with pathos the demise of the epoch of the shipyards and the effects on the workers. *Major Operation* relates a comparative study in class difference and reconciliation, and the effects of unemployment on the shipyard workers and bankrupt businessmen alike. *No Mean City* reveals, and seemingly revels in, the social degradation and criminal underclass created by the development of capitalism in Glasgow.

This last novel alone of the genre attempts no historical materialist analysis of contemporary political conditions in the city and, like *The Shipbuilders*, it occasionally disparages but mostly ignores, the left-wing politics, the unions, and the unemployed workers' movement that so dominated the politics of Glasgow at the time; an omission which may suggest conservative political leanings in the authors.

There has been some contention regarding the class credentials of the writers of the so-called proletariat Glasgow novels and their ability to speak legitimately for the working class. In a series of articles discussing the working class novel in Scotland, Mitchell, focusing on the period 1900-1939, critiques the prevalence of what he refers to as the 'pseudo-working class novel ... one of the achievements of decadent bourgeois literature in the twentieth century'.[84] Of the five writers under consideration, it is only James Barke's working class background and Marxist communism that provide sufficient authority and authenticity to qualify as genuinely 'working class' in Mitchell's opinion. He commends *Major Operation* as 'a heroic attempt to lay, almost single-handed, the foundations for the proletarian socialist-realist novel in Scotland'.[85] Barke was a Glasgow shipyard worker from a farm worker's family, who wrote a number of novels about Scotland; and *Major Operation* contains powerfully realistic descriptions of the unemployed workers' movement and industrial unrest in inter-war Glasgow, informed by his knowledge of the city and sympathy with the labour movement. However the writers of the other four novels do not possess Mitchell's requisite qualifications for producing a genuine proletariat novel. Dot Allan (*Hunger March*) was a nurse and freelance writer from a Glasgow merchant family. Alexander McArthur (*No Mean City*) was a working class baker from the Gorbals who had written other novels, but only published this one before ending his own life.[86] His co-writer H. Kingsley Long, whose opinions dominate *No Mean City*, was a middle class London journalist. George Blake (*The Shipbuilders*) was a middle class journalist and literary critic from Greenock, who wrote a substantial number of non-fiction texts

---

84 Jack Mitchell 'The struggle for the working class novel in Scotland'. p.40.
85 Mitchell, Ibid. p.42.
86 For a fuller account of Alexander McArthur and *No Mean City* see Seán Damer. 'No Mean Writer? The Curious Case of Alexander McArthur', in Kevin McCarra and Hamish Whyte (eds), *A Glasgow Collection: Essays in Honour of Joe Fisher.* (Glasgow City Libraries: Glasgow,1990).

and novels concerning Glasgow. Edward Shiels (*Gael Over Glasgow*) remains something of a mystery, described by the *Glasgow Herald* as 'a Clydebank man and an engineer who has been incapacitated by an accident', he died young after writing only the one novel, for which the *Herald* commended him (in the same article) for his first hand knowledge of the shipyards.[87] The possibility that Shiels may also have been a working class shipyard engineer like the hero of his novel would surely have provided him the credentials to qualify as a 'genuinely working class writer'. However there are indications in his novel that he may have come from more middle class origins.

The Glasgow realist novels occasionally attempt a Modernist strategy with varying success. There are long stream of consciousness passages in *Major Operation* and *No Mean City* in which the realistic narrative is punctuated with political and economic analysis intended to reflect the collective voice of the Glasgow Everyman. However the novels are at their best when describing events in a realistic journalistic fashion, a style prevalent at a time when English journalists were being shown around Glasgow's poor areas as a sort of sideshow.[88] George Blake was a journalist, and perhaps consequently *The Shipbuilders* expresses overt awareness of the power of journalism, with references to the characters reliance on the press to mediate their world: 'Danny did not really understand it until he read his evening paper on the way home'. (SH, p.70) This is particularly interesting with reference to how the press were considered partly responsible, along with the police, for the creation of popular perceptions of the dominance of gangs and Red Clydeside in Glasgow during the inter-war era.

The city of Glasgow itself functions as a protagonist in all the novels, (discussed in Chapter Three). *Hunger March* does not refer to Glasgow by name but the characteristics of the city are obvious. Similarly *Major Operation* refers obliquely to the 'The Second City' or 'the City', although streets and places in Glasgow are referred to by their given names. This invocation to the Second City in *Major Operation* runs like a refrain throughout the text from the lyrical opening: 'The sun set over the Second City. The Second City of the Empire on which the sun never sets'; (MO, p.13) and similarly in *No Mean City*, there are repeated ironic references to Glasgow's former glory as the 'Empire's Second City'. The novels all, to varying degrees,

87 *Glasgow Herald*, 5 March, 1937, pers.comm from Seán Damer June 2010.
88 Slum tourism as part of the vogue for travel writing in the 1920s and 1930s.

comment on the irony of the continuing myth of Glasgow as Second City of Empire after its economic decline; all contain elements of pathos and nostalgia for the city's past glory, and a sense of incomprehension at its sudden reversal of fortune. Francis Russell Hart asks: 'How did the mighty fall? It is a sop for Calvinist morality...The economic shift seemed so sudden and drastic as to invite superstitious awe and tragic saga'.[89] And it is the lapse and liminality of this once great city that is caught for posterity in the five inter-war realist novels.

Five Forgotten Novels of Glasgow

The inter-war era was an important period for Glasgow fiction at a moment when capitalism was clearly in crisis, and writers were anxious to explore creatively the social and political significance of this apparent economic failure. The First World War provided a nexus of liminality; it was the catalyst for shaking up the old certainties about Glasgow and contributing to a climate of negativity. Previously existing problems assumed a new resonance. There was also a crisis of confidence in the British State in the 1930s, and the prediction of the end of capitalism. The Glasgow realist writers tried to explain in fiction what was happening and what to do about it.

The five inter-war realist novels are historically and geographically specific. The industrial powerhouse that was Glasgow underwent massive changes in response to the changing global economy after the First World War. In addition to the economic and political context, the novels occurred at the same time as the cultural movement towards a Scottish Renaissance, itself an endeavour to critique the nation and its ills. The popular view of Glasgow as Second City vied with the mystique of Red Clydeside. The novels attempt to delineate the conditions existing within the city at the time, primarily focusing upon the working classes, and can be regarded within a framework of new urban realism, arising from a desire to move from the romanticised Kailyard tropes preceding them. In doing so, they present a valuable historical record of Glasgow within a defining liminal moment in its history.

However four of the novels examined here have not survived to become part of a literary canon. Like the shipyards themselves, the Clydebuilt novels have disappeared without leaving much trace. The novels were presumably written for a highly literate readership in

---

89 Francis Russell Hart, *The Scottish Novel from Smollett to Spark*. (Harvard University Press: Cambridge Massachusetts, 1978) p.205.

Glasgow, and when first published they were iconic examples of the realistic genre, summing up the city in the popular consciousness. Seven decades later most of the novels are difficult to obtain. *The Shipbuilders* has been reprinted in paperback and is available for sale online and in Glasgow's second hand bookstores; *Major Operation* underwent one reprinting in 1955 during the height of the popularity of Barke's novels on Robert Burns, but now along with *Hunger March* and *Gael Over Glasgow* neither of which were published again, these novels are available to read only as reference copies in Glasgow's Mitchell Library, or occasionally obtainable for sale online. [90]

The incongruous anomaly in this scenario of abandonment is *No Mean City*, probably *the* Glasgow novel best known to the general public. It became an instant best seller when published, has never been out of print, and is the only 1930s Glasgow realist novel still available and in demand seventy years later. However this novel has caused much controversy and objection to its depiction of Glasgow, standing accused of stigmatising the city and creating the dark stereotype of 'Violent' and 'Depressed' Glasgow; an enduring popular image of the city until the 1980s, emulated in other fictional depictions. This account is however no longer pertinent, either in literary terms or in the social reality of the city. Gradually the perceptions and representations of Glasgow are becoming disentangled from that of degradation and aggression[91].

Possible reasons are discussed in Chapter Six for why these novels, which represent Glasgow so realistically during the inter-war era, have mostly been ignored by critics and publishers; reduced like the city to a state of permanent liminality. Were the novels designed to entertain an audience whose tastes have since changed? Eagleton argues that realism in general went out of fashion because:

> the ordinary reader delights in the exotic and extravagant. The irony is that the novel as a form is wedded to the common life, whereas the common people themselves prefer the monstrous and miraculous ... do not wish to see their own faces in the mirror of art. They have quite enough ordinary life in their working hours without wanting to contemplate it in their leisure time as well. Labourers are more likely to resort to fantasy than lawyers.'[92]

---

90 In 2010 the Association for Scottish Literary Studies republished *Hunger March* in the same volume with another novel by Dot Allan. *Makeshift*, (edited by Moira Burgess).

91 Much as the Clyde is getting cleaner too.

92 Eagleton, *The English Novel: An Introduction*. p.5

Were the novels written to provide a synopsis of Glasgow at a time which, only in retrospect, can be perceived as an historical watershed in the evolution of the city? Is it that they lack sufficient social comment to be regarded as historical documents, or are deficient in enough literary merit to survive as scholarly works? Academic analysis tends to change with time – each new era producing differing readings. Is it merely that the theoretical approaches of previous scholars have not been suitable to garner any relevant rewards from a critique of the novels? Is it that these novels did not comply with literary critiques which were fashioned to fit the agenda of their authors? The attempts at social realism mixed with romanticism evinced in the novels do not fall into the category of Kailyard, nor do they fit easily within a paradigm of pure social realism. The novels perhaps could be viewed as a 'missing link' – an evolutionary literary step which has yet to be identified?

Although now difficult to obtain, the novels have continuing relevance in that they provide a realistic socio-historical record of inter-war Glasgow. The question that may need to be asked by anyone interested in the promotion of Scottish literature is: why have these novels been marginalised? Possible answers may lie in the changing marketing strategies of publishers, a history of reader reception, fashions in literary styles, gate-keeping by literary critics and publicists, or a sense of discomfort with their message. Perhaps many of the novels succeed more as social representation and commentary than they do as literary texts. Their appeal may have been limited precisely because of their specific sense of time and place. However it is because of their very value as realistic historical documents that a case can be made for their publication revival. So an attempt is made here to discover why so few of these novels have been re-published, and so perhaps uncover a silence in Scottish history, possibly recover a lost voice in Scottish literature.

2   City in Crisis

Inter-war Economy and the Great Depression

Introduction

Glasgow retained its powerful Second City of Empire status until the second decade of the twentieth century. But the city's export-reliant economy depended on an expanding world market and, due to realigning forces of economic globalisation and trade protectionism, the global economy began contracting after the First World War.[1] Subsequently the post-war recession of the 1920s developed into the major economic crisis of the Great Depression in the 1930s. Clydeside was one of the worst affected areas in Britain because of the overly specialised nature of its industry and workforce, and its related inability to adapt to changing global demands. These factors contributed to the increasing irrelevance of Glasgow within the world production markets, resulting in the closure of industries, the unemployment of the work force, and the decline of the city's infrastructure. It was the start of a downward spiral from which the city's export economy never recovered.

The claim to realism of the five Glasgow novels examined here requires that they should accurately reflect the seismic shifts in the economic landscape, and the effects upon the protagonists and the social life of the city during the inter-war era. This chapter examines what the novels and the Condition of Scotland discourse reveal about the crisis of capitalism during this time; and the reasons provided for the economic decline of Glasgow as Second City of Empire. It also looks at how realistically the novels document the social and political consequences of these events when compared with contemporaneous non-fiction writing about the city.

---

1   Alan Massie, *Portraits of a City,* Barrie and Jenkins (London, 1989), p.99.

Local Responses to Global Trends

Analysis of the inter-war crisis of capitalism and how it affected Scotland failed, at the time it was happening, to appreciate the deep-rooted structural weaknesses in the Scottish economic system. The new global economic order was one in which access to technology, electric power, markets and financial centres, and cheaper labour; became more important than Glasgow's traditional assets of proximity to raw materials and a skilled labour force. Glasgow's economy had become dependent on heavy industry and shipbuilding, which relocated elsewhere in the world as the twentieth century progressed. These changes were initially artificially delayed by the approach and onset of the Second World War. However the revolution in the global economic system accelerated from 1945 onwards — an era characterised by British industrial and imperial decline. The relentless dynamic of rapidly restructuring capital was inevitably to result in the redundancy and unemployment of large numbers of workers in the labour-intensive heavy manufacturing, engineering and shipbuilding economy of Clydeside; and in the ultimate demise of those industries.

After the First World War, under conditions of disarmament, all new and existing military shipbuilding contracts were suspended for ten years. Subsequently Glasgow's dominance of shipbuilding was challenged by Japan and the United States. Faced with a declining world market for their products, Glasgow industrialists did not move quickly enough to adapt to the changing economic order. Irene Maver makes the important point that the problem was compounded by the continued reliance of Clyde shipbuilders on an outmoded form of technology, the marine steam engine, as opposed to the state-of-the-art diesel engine, at a time when radically new methods of organization were necessary to compete internationally.[2] The fluctuations of Clyde shipbuilding output went from 'over 672,000 tons in 1920 ....to the unprecedented nadir of 56,000 in 1933'.[3] This ebb and flow of supply and demand in the Clyde shipbuilding industry and its ultimate demise is ably illustrated in *The Shipbuilders*. The novel describes the declining fortunes of the Clyde in the parallel lives of protagonists Leslie Pagan shipyard owner and his employee

---

2   Irene Maver, *Glasgow* (Edinburgh University Press: Edinburgh, 2000),p.205.
3   J.Cunnison and J.B.S. Gilfillian (eds), *Glasgow: the third statistical account of Scotland,* (Collins: Glasgow 1958), p. 841.

and old war comrade Danny Shields the shipyard riveter, as it documents the ending of the era of pride in 'Clyde-built' due to: 'the fantastic shrinkage of world trade; the development of building abroad; state subsidies to foreign builders and owners; the ghastly mess of currencies'. (SH, p.3)

Attempts to salvage the shipyards during the inter-war era were largely futile. Sir James Lithgow, one of the great shipbuilding patriarchs, formed the National Shipbuilders Security Limited (NSS) in the 1930s as an attempt to rationalise and streamline declining industries. The NSS acquired and closed Beardmore's, and within three years a further half-dozen Clyde yards had ceased operations, two had suspended work, and three were operating on restricted quotas.[4] In *The Shipbuilders* the refrain, 'Not a single order on the books', is repeated throughout the first chapter as Leslie struggles to understand, 'the economy of a world gone mad'. (SH, p.11) His attempts to procure new orders from London prove futile. Not even his old boys' network connections can save his shipyard as he learns from a ship owner acquaintance's irate and prophetic response to his request for orders: 'Ships! There are too many damned ships in the world just now, and too damned little to put into them. ....it's going to get worse. ... Not a hope for us for years, if then, with all this tommyrot of tariffs and subsidies.' (SH, p.108) Leslie comes to understand that: 'A strange, mocking fatalism had settled on the world of shipping. No trade, and the Government talking either economy or disarmament, and hence no ships of war'. (SH, p.108)

In *Gael Over Glasgow*, after the completion and launch of the last ship to be built in Beardmore's the shipyard is empty. The hopelessness of the situation is described in numerous passages: 'things were at a standstill in the shipbuilding industry and likely to remain so. The foreigners were building their own ships and disarmament had robbed the Clyde of its largest orders'; (GG, p.286) and, 'It seemed that Big Business awaited the result of this latest war between Capital and Labour before embarking on any new ventures'. (GG, p.221)

When they are made redundant ('the pay-off') the shipyard workers in the novel realise they may not get work again anywhere in the present economic situation:

---

4   Anthony Slaven, *The Development of the West of Scotland 1750-1960* (Routledge & Paul Kegan: London, 1975), p.189.

A pay-off was nothing unusual in this life, but now with this crisis facing Society, and unprecedented industrial stagnation, who could hope for work again?...Was the Clyde's greatness ended? ... on all sides one heard the continually reiterated statement that Capitalism was finished and had to go. (GG, pp.230-231)

The narrative of *The Shipbuilders* opens with the launch of the last ship to be built by the fictional firm of Pagan's, its maiden voyage down the Clyde providing a vehicle for a passage of pathos eulogising the Clyde shipbuilding industry: 'the high, tragic pageant of the Clyde'. (SH, p.118) A pseudo-Homeric litany listing the lost shipyards follows the last Pagan's ship as it moves down towards the Clyde Firth, documenting the 'grim majesty of the parade' of now defunct shipyards, presented in names which correspond to historical reality. Leslie laments the demise of the Clyde as 'a catastrophe unthinkable' (SH, p.119) as nostalgically he imagines the history of the great river: 'Out of this narrow river they had poured, an endless pageant, to fill the ports of the world'. (SH, p.121) The narrative is prophetic in that Leslie's liberal conscience is appalled at the thought of how many of the shipyard workers will never work again, at the loss of skills never to be regained, but more so by the sense of waste inherent in the decline of the industry itself:

It was a tragedy beyond economics ... a tradition, a skill, a glory, a passion, was visibly in decay and all the acquired and inherited loveliness of artistry rotting along the banks of the stream... as if shipbuilding man had tried to do too much and had been defeated by his own conception. (SH, pp.118-119)

The narrative voice creates a sense of the heroic hubris of the scene rising to a crescendo of hyperbolic portent:

It was as if a race had worshipped grim gods of the sea. And now the tide had turned back...Never again would the Clyde be what it had been...The fall of Rome was a trifle in comparison...the collapse of a dynasty or the defeat of a great nation in battle was a transient disturbance. (SH, p.121)

Fluctuations in Glasgow's economic fortunes, the varying and inadequate responses from the government and business community, and the 'mounting sense of insecurity in the city' during the inter-war years, are examined by Maver, who posits that technical advances made during the First World War should have presented opportunities for economic diversification in Glasgow's industries, particularly in the area of aircraft production.[5] The continuing reliance of Glasgow on heavy industry, and the decline of its fortunes, are noted by Edwin Muir in *Scottish Journey* (1935), an insightful account of the economic, social and political consequences of industrialisation on Scotland:

> Scottish iron is almost at a standstill; coal is declining; and shipping and shipbuilding in Britain generally have sunk so definitely that not even optimists expect them to be again what they once were, except in the event of another war. The probable consequence seems to be that Glasgow, after its rapid expansion, is fated to shrink again.[6]

Muir's analysis of the crisis of capitalism in Scotland is largely concerned with Glasgow, the city he considered to be the most representative of industrialised Scotland:[7] 'In one way it may be said that Glasgow *is* modern Scotland, since it is the most active and vital part of Scotland as well as the most populous'.[8] Scotland's problems were blamed on England by nationalists such as George Malcolm Thomson and Andrew Dewar Gibb, who compared the post-war recovery of the Scottish economy unfavourably with the situation in England: 'Scotland is to-day, ... very much less prosperous than England ... Scotland suffers more than England. The proportion of persons unemployed in Scotland is consistently higher than it is in England'.[9] *Major Operation* articulates the effects of the fluctuations in the inter-war economy on the Glasgow business community, 'Throughout the City there was hardship. Bankruptcies, sequestrations and liquidations were the order of the day. Business men failed right and left', (MO, p.375) culminating in the bankruptcy of protagonist George Anderson. The uneven and contradictory nature of the effects of the economic depression on business is also documented in the novel: 'Here and there profits continued to mount

---

5   Maver, *Glasgow*, p.203.
6   Edwin Muir, *Scottish Journey*, (Mainstream Publishing Company: Edinburgh, 1935:1979) p.128.
7   Ibid., p.98.
8   Ibid,, p.102.
9   Andrew Dewar Gibb, *Scotland in Eclipse*, (Humphrey Toulmin: London,1930), p.65-69.

and swell'; (MO, p.375) but, 'there were businesses that seemed to flourish, depression or no depression. Luxury trades: the radio trade, for example'. (MO, p.237)

Another of the novels, *Hunger March*, describes a twenty-four hour period in Glasgow, the day of the 'All Scotland Hunger March', which occurs on the very day that Glasgow entrepreneur Arthur Joyce has chosen to close down his business 'Joyce and Son — India merchants' and 'there was some talk ... that if trade didn't look up his would be the next big firm to find itself in Queer Street.' (HM, p.39) *Hunger March* also overtly critiques the culpability of the owners of the means of production, who chose to close down their businesses making their workers redundant rather than struggle on and stay open throughout the economic crisis. A clerk working for Arthur Joyce thinks: 'damn all the craven firms that hadn't faced the Depression, fought it out!' (HM, p.66) But in *Major Operation*, the hopeful signs that the economy is picking up and the worst of the Depression may be over are depicted as an aspect of false consciousness: 'Superficial signs that the middle class, in their complete ignorance of the economic structure of society, did not understand'. (MO, p.238) On the other hand, *The Shipbuilders* portrays the workers as being the ones with the hopeful belief that the situation must get better. After one of the main characters Danny the riveter becomes unemployed, he believes that life and work will return to normal: 'he clung to a strong and almost mystic faith that he was only marking time until, shortly, he would be back with the squad at the hammer, holder-on and mate and rivet-boy in a happy solidarity of work'.(SH, p.97) Brian the engineer in *Gael Over Glasgow* projects his own ideological mystification onto that of the trade union movement:

> There was a great deal of confusion even amongst the workers' leaders ...They did not know what was the real cause of the distress and to what extent the crisis would develop. But the War and Capitalism was enough to go on with. (GG, p.107)

In *Scottish Scene*, Lewis Grassic Gibbon begins a chapter entitled 'Glasgow', by quoting from his earlier text in which he describes the city as 'the vomit of a cataleptic commercialism', a theme which he expands upon here:

> Commercialism has returned to its own vomit too often and too long still to find sustenance therein... in Glasgow (as elsewhere) they call

this condition "The Crisis" .... the remedy lies neither in medicine nor massage, but in surgery.[10]

And the need for surgery as a response to Glasgow's ills is expanded in *Major Operation* which elaborates and dissects the sustained trope of the sick city needing economic surgery:

> The crisis continued to eat into the economic life, the basic structure of the Second City. The once red pulsating blood of the City was impoverished: it dripped grey like the rain. The social reflection of the crisis was equally grey. There were many surgeons round the bedside of the City: there were anaesthetists and there were nurses....But nothing could stem the grey blood from dripping. The patient was sinking. (MO, p.228)

The Glasgow economy was designed for, and dominated by, heavy industrial production. Therefore, with the growing anticipation of the Second World War, new armaments production became the projected panacea for the economic problems of the inter-war era. This is a situation ironically commented upon in *Major Operation*: 'Everything had gone with a bang during the last war. Things might go with a bigger bang during the next war. Fortunes had been made in the last: greater fortunes might be made in the next.'(MO, p.237) Preparations for the Second World War began in Glasgow in 1936, and unemployment figures fell as workers were drawn back into industry and the military. However, although the Glasgow economy was briefly rejuvenated just prior to, and for the duration of, the war period, there were underlying problems that would resurface after 1945.

The Clyde Shipyards

Clydeside was once the shipbuilding centre of the world, and 'as late as the 1950's the river was still producing approximately one seventh of the total tonnage of sea-going ships in the world'.[11] Given the fact that shipbuilding in Glasgow was still a major industry until midway through the twentieth century, it is surprising that some of the realist novels so dramatically document the demise of the

---

10 Lewis Grassic Gibbon, *Scottish Scene*. (Cedric Chivers: Bath. 1934:1974), p.143.
11 Brian Osborne and others, *Glasgow's River* (Lindsay Publications: Glasgow, 1996), p.58.

shipyards during the inter-war era. However this can be attributed to the fluctuating nature of the Clydeside economy and the brief recovery of the shipyards through rearmament for the Second World War starting in 1936; so the effects would only have become apparent after all five novels had been written.

It must also be remembered that actual shipbuilding formed only a relatively small sector of Glasgow's economy, employing a minor percentage of the industrial workforce in comparison with the heavy engineering and metal-working industries. However a great range of Glasgow's subsidiary industries were tied into supplying the needs of the shipbuilders.[12] Clyde shipbuilding often acted as a cipher and allegory for the health of Glasgow: when shipbuilding thrived Glasgow prospered. Therefore the closure of the shipyards during the inter-war era was to affect the entire economy of Glasgow, and the demise of the Clyde industry was significant to the mythology and morale of a city intrinsically enmeshed with the identity of its river. The symbolism and mythology of the Clyde runs omnipresently through two of the novels, glorifying and documenting for posterity the history of epic shipbuilding. *The Shipbuilders* functions as an elegy to the lost shipyards along the length of the Clyde, and *Gael Over Glasgow* historically links the working life and proletarian politics of the Clydebank shipyards with those of Glasgow.

The complex internal stratification of the Glasgow industrial working class[13] is described by Seán Damer as, 'fissured-more deeply than any other in Britain, by skill, gender, religion, and regularity of employment'.[14] Summarised here is his categorisation of the layers of the labour hierarchy in the shipbuilding industry, the skilled and better paid jobs being the preserve of Protestants with the lower status jobs being left to Irish and Highlanders: skilled labour – engineers, pattern-makers, boiler-makers; also skilled — tradesmen, iron and brass-moulders, shipwrights, joiners, blacksmiths, hammermen, plumbers, riggers; classified as semi-skilled — the 'black Squad', riveters, holders-on, platers, anglesmiths and caulkers; so-called unskilled — seasonal and casualised labouring jobs requiring

---

12 Maver, *Glasgow,* p.120.

13 see *The Bowler and the Bunnet,* a 1967 documentary directed by Sean Connery re stratification in the Glasgow shipyards .

14 Seán Damer, *Glasgow — Going for a Song* (Lawrence & Wishart Ltd: London,1990).p.58.

strength and stamina, but containing a wide range of skills including stevedoring and red-leading.[15]

Three of the inter-war novels provide an idea of the work of the shipyards, and the hierarchical nature of their organisation, with job status and specification firmly established. *Major Operation* details the work of 'the red leaders' scraping the ship's plates with wire brushes and repainting it, hanging all the while from the ship sides in 'flat punts'. The work was difficult, dirty and dangerous and the paint extremely toxic: 'To swing a paint brush in ordinary paint is a tiresome job; to swing heavy red-lead over a rough surface is worse. But to swing a heavy brush on the end of pole requires great effort and long practice'. (MO, p.45) Of all the inter-war novels, *Gael Over Glasgow* contains the most detailed realistic descriptions of shipyard work at a particular time in history, so serving as a worthy documentary. It describes 'the black squad', who tacked the plates of the ship together with bolts and brute force before the advent of welding: 'unmistakable with their dirty faces and stained clothes, the riveters, caulkers, holeborers and platers, the men who cut, bend and build the frame and hull of the ship.'(GG, p.335) The narrative explains in loving detail the work of a now largely lost skill.

> a riveter grasped a red hot rivet in expert tongs and inserted it into a hole in the bulkhead plates. A bump from his heavy pneumatic hammer splashed sparks again as the rivet was bashed close up to the plate. Then the riveter braced himself for the kick of his hammer, the hanging plank on which he stood swinging out dangerously. Suddenly, from the other side of the bulkhead, came the roar of a pneumatic hammer battering at the front of the rivet, while the man above Brian gritted his teeth and hung on to his dancing hammer. (GG, p.20)

The changing economic dynamics of the shipyards and the effects of modernization and progress are articulated in *The Shipbuilders*. The riveters are already being replaced with the advent of the new technology of welding:

> Now in the place of the riveter was the welder, joining the plates of ships with a melting jet of white flame; and no riveter of the old school could hope to graduate in the fierce new art. Now one man and a boy,

---

15 From Damer. Ibid. p.59

working a machine, could do in the way of making hatches what it used to take fourteen craftsmen to do ... One man, commanding a single drill-punch, displaced six of his kind ... the number of men in the yards fell by one half in the ten years from 1920 – and would go on falling. (SH, p.264)

The hellish world of heavy industry is romanticised in *Gael Over Glasgow*. There is a sense of the ability to have godlike collective control of the elements versus the frailty of individual humanity. The birth of giant ships is being described, so the imagery is gargantuan, with men tiny in comparison, evocative of a Muirhead Bone etching. The noise in the shipyards must have been deafening, 'the sustained snarl of pneumatic caulking machines from the close staccato or the riveting hammers in the shipyards of Brown's and Beardmore's'. (GG, p.1) Other than in the opening chapters, most of *Major Operation* and *The Shipbuilders* describe a Clydeside in which the shipbuilding work has already departed, although the latter text repeatedly evokes the nostalgic imagery of the previously industrious Clydeside:

In the great days, there was not one of these yards but had two or three big ships a-building, so that up and down the River the bows of vessels unlaunched towered over the tenement buildings of the workers and people passing could hardly hear themselves speak for the clangor of metal upon metal that filled the valley from Old Kilpatrick up to Govan. (SH, p.47)

The Second Clearances

In a process beginning with the transference of political power to London after the Union of the Scots with the English Parliament in 1707, the control of Scotland's economy shifted relentlessly southwards over the years. The Condition of Scotland writers were particularly critical of this trend, known in the 1930s as 'the southward drift of industry', a tendency that has continued even into the twenty-first-century. George Malcolm Thomson in *Caledonia or the Future of the Scots* laments the southward migration of business and skill from Glasgow:

a general process of removing the control of Scottish administration, commerce, and industry four hundred miles further South...The head offices of shipping companies which once were crowded together in

Glasgow no longer fly their house-flags in St Vincent Street. They are mostly transferred South of the Border to London or Liverpool. ....One immediate result of this tendency is to give increased impetus to a form of emigration from the country ... the drain of the educated, intelligent, and energetic middle class youth who would normally become the leaders of the commercial, political and intellectual life of the country.[16]

Thomson maintained that moving the control of business and industry to London, far from Scotland, made economic decision-making difficult and inefficient: 'Not only is Scottish industry decaying, it is steadily ceasing to be Scottish. Four out of eight banks having been affiliated to English banks ... Scottish railways are now directed from London'.[17] Some of the problems Thomson lists regarding the state of the economy in Scotland of the 1920s are similar to the issues of the early twenty-first-century, although there have been changes since devolution. The subservient economic position of Scotland to England, the seeming irrationality of the movement towards the metropolis, and the social consequences for Scotland are protested by Andrew Dewar Gibb in *Scotland in Eclipse*:

Great commercial concerns have flitted their offices, lock, stock and barrel to London or elsewhere in England. The reason apparently alleged is that they must be near the centre of things if they are to compete with their rivals... it is amazing that it should be necessary at a time of day when people can communicate with one another over long distances more easily than ever before....Instances of total closure are to be found in the shipyards, in the chemical and sugar-refining industries, in agriculture, in the railway workshops, in the textile trade ... More and more of the great shops and stores pass under English control ... Every step in these disastrous processes means more unemployment, more misery, and more emigration for Scotsmen.[18]

Following the movement of industry, skilled labour in Scotland was drawn south towards London in a mass migration referred to in the 1930s and in *Gael Over Glasgow* as 'the Second Clearances'.(GG, p.332) When Brian's friends in *Gael Over Glasgow* move to London in

16 George Malcolm Thomson, *Caledonia or the Future of the Scots* (Paul Kegan: London, 1927) p.47-51.
17 Thomson, Ibid, pp.47-51.
18 Gibb, *Scotland in Eclipse*, p.65-69.

search of employment they inform him, 'There's thousands of young men leaving the country for England every week', (GG, p.331) and 'From Glasgow and the distressed areas young men, cut off without any means of support by the Means Test, were leaving their homes for London where the light industries were booming'.(GG, p.332) In a critical polemic directed against the inability of Scotland to retain its talented skilled population, Muir describes the decanting of the nation thus:

> Scotland is gradually being emptied of its population, its spirit, its wealth, industry, art, intellect and innate character. This is a sad conclusion; but it has some support on historical grounds. If a country exports its most enterprising spirits and best minds year after year, for fifty or a hundred or two hundred years, some result will inevitably follow.[19]

Edmund Stegmaier asserts that the emphasis in the economic analyses of the inter-war era was on statistics and 'fact'.[20] In 1935 Thomson published another tract on the condition of Scotland entitled *That Distressed Area*,[21] wherein he uses statistics to compare the economic development of Scotland with that of England and nine other European countries with roughly the same population as Scotland at the time. Between 1913 and 1930 the figures for Scotland indicate greater decline in population, higher unemployment, lower national income, decrease in volume of industrial production, decline in basic industries and failure to initiate new secondary industries. In his review Muir considers *That Distressed Area* to be the first text to successfully define 'the Scottish Question' and the economic state of Scotland. He applauds Thomson's conclusion that: 'The character of the Scottish problem is that of stealth, of gradual attrition of physical and economic resources, of a decline in strength which is only perceptible over comparatively long periods'.[22]

---

19 Edwin Muir, *Scottish Journey*, pp. 3-4.
20 Edmund Stegmaier, 'Facts and Vision in Scottish Writing of the 1920s and 1930s'. *Scottish Literary Journal*, 9, Nov 1982, pp.67-78.
21 George Malcolm Thomson, *Scotland: That Distressed Area* (Porpoise Press: Edinburgh, 1935).
22 Edwin Muir :1979 'Review of George Malcolm Thomson', *Criterion* (Jan, 1936), pp.330-32.

Unemployment and the Reserve Army of Labour

During the inter-war era Scotland had an unemployment rate 50% higher than England, and average wages for those who were in work was consistently lower.[23] Scotland's industrial success had been to a great extent due to competitive pricing at the expense of workers' wages — paid six times less than in England. Labour was hired on a casual basis, and subject to one hour's notice only.[24] These labour practices were exploitative and caused resentment and mistrust given the vast wealth being generated by the workers for the owners of the means of production. A 1934 survey indicated the percentage of United Kingdom populations in the top income bracket earning more than £10 per week: England average 5%, Edinburgh 7%, Glasgow 2%.[25] A 1936 survey indicated the percentage of the workforce unemployed in cities in the United Kingdom: London 10%, Edinburgh 14%, Glasgow 29%.[26] Unemployment in Glasgow rose to unprecedented levels at the worst time of the Great Depression.[27]

The five realist novels all illustrate the effects on inter-war Glasgow of the increase in unemployment, and the decrease in real wages for those who managed to keep their jobs; along with the attendant increase in poverty, alienation and anomie in the social conditions of the working class. Ingrained in Glaswegian collective memory are the well-documented scenes of depressed, demoralised, disempowered men hanging around on street corners, waiting in dole queues, a reserve army of labour to be used or rejected as needed by the owners of the means of production. The anxiety about, as well as the actuality of, unemployment, and its effects on the morale and mental health of the work force during the Depression, dominated the zeitgeist of the city at the time and informs all five of the realistic Glasgow novels. It is evoked by Ralph Glasser in his memories of the daily scene outside Dixon's Blazes blast furnace just south of the Gorbals:

---

23 George Malcolm Thomson, *Caledonia or the Future of the Scots*, pp.26-46.
24 The Clyde shipbuilding firms also did not pay for training their workers, which was all done through apprenticeship on the job.
25 M. Abrams, *Home Market.* (London,1937). pp. 10-20
26 Ibid.
27 Not only Glasgow but other 'special areas' of the UK that concentrated on mining, steel and shipbuilding were also badly affected – see Wal Hannington, *The Problem of the Distressed Areas* (Victor Gollanz: London, 1937).

Outside the twenty-foot high gates were clustered a couple of dozen men in cloth caps, fustian jackets and mufflers, heavy black trousers tied with string below the knees. Lantern-jawed, saturnine, faces glazed with cold, collars turned up under their ears and heads bowed, they stood huddled in upon themselves, sheltering within their own bodies, as sheep do on a storm-swept hillside.[28]

A reserve army of labour is required for a capitalist system to work effectively, a pool of unemployed workers to be drawn upon when business is booming and extra production is needed to meet demand. When not required these workers were cut loose to fend for themselves as best they could until the introduction of social security or 'the dole' in the United Kingdom. The insecurity of this situation is documented in *Major Operation*: 'There was the haunting fear of unemployment ... they lived in the midst of it. Few in South Partick could boast of regular employment. There were men who had never done a stroke of work in years'.(MO, p.79) Competition between workers for scarce jobs and the resulting fear of unemployment and demoralisation of the work force sustains low wages in such a situation. The degrading poverty of this condition is depicted in *Major Operation*, where during an unemployment protest the workers in their ragged clothes are described as 'The Second City's waste human labour'. (MO, p.128)

The economic insecurity induced by too few jobs for too many workers is an understanding expressed in *Major Operation*. When he is still a business owner, George Anderson holds a bourgeois perspective on unemployment and, believing in the myth of the meritocracy, he cannot comprehend that work is unavailable to those who try hard enough to find it. However by the time George has lost his own livelihood due to the vagaries of capitalism, he is ready to listen to Jock MacKelvie, the socialist worker leader he meets in hospital, who 'puts him right'. Jock himself has been unemployed for seven years. He has experienced: 'four years' intermittent unemployment: three years' steady unemployment ... Seven years of hardship and bitterness'. Moreover Jock has not wasted his time during his enforced idleness, participating in 'seven years of intensive self-education and discipline'. (MO, p.130) This is a reference to the night schools organised by the Socialists in Glasgow

---

28 Ralph Glasser, *Growing up in the Gorbals*, (Edinburgh: Black & White Publishing, 2006), p.6.

at the time, and Jock's analysis of the situation is informed by an understanding of Marxist economics. He enlightens George as to the reality of the economic situation during a crisis of capitalism: 'There are over three million unemployed in this country. But there aren't three million jobs waiting to be filled. ...Capitalism can't and never will be able to absorb the unemployed. And the capitalist state can't and never will be able to guarantee their dependants more than a bare existence.' (MO, p.337) Jock's hard lesson in economic reality includes a reminder to the now unemployed George, who has few skills other than managerial, that 'there are thousands of men and women in this City in a much better position to take work than you are: clerks, typists, book-keepers, accountants: they can't get work though they've been trying for years'. (MO, p.336) When Jock had realized he would probably never be fully employed again he joined the unemployed movement. He encourages George to do likewise, and the re-education of bourgeois George is the vehicle for the political discussion and rhetoric throughout the novel, conveying presumably the Marxist sentiments of the author James Barke.

As the economic situation worsens in *Gael Over Glasgow*, 'pay-off day' becomes increasingly inevitable at the Beardmore's shipyard where workers try to invent jobs for themselves to avoid it. Eventually 'The foreman came down the stairs at last with a list in his hand ... Men bent over their jobs and made a passable pretence of feverish industry'. Brian too is laid off, told to 'finish up' and 'get ashore and get your insurance books and lying time at the dock office'.(GG, pp.228-230) After much searching Brian finds employment at John Brown's shipyard in Clydebank, 'now known all over the world as the builders of the famous Queen Mary', the ship iconically known as Cunarder Number 534 on Clydeside during the 1930s.(GG, p.334) However this historic shipyard was also to experience an enforced work hiatus due to economic exigencies. The irrationality and immorality of this situation is depicted in the memoirs of David Kirkwood, Red Clydesider and Labour MP, who articulates his outrage at the waste of the highly-skilled Clyde workforce and the undermining of a proud work ethic:

> For more than two years the Clyde had been like a tomb. Not a tomb newly made, but a tomb with a vast and inescapable skeleton brooding over its silence. For two years that gaunt frame had stood lifeless. It had sapped the vitality from a great town – aye, from a

nation. Beneath its shadow men have crept about battered and broken by enforced idleness. These men – the finest, the most expert craftsmen in the world – had lived their lives in their work. [29]

In *The Shipbuilders*, pay-off day at Pagan's shipyard is described in a paternalistic passage of pathos. As Leslie Pagan observes his workers leaving the yard for the last time: 'streaming noiselessly towards the gate, the crowds of men who were to lift their last pay as they went out', he wonders whether this was worse than the suffering he had experienced with his men in the trenches during the First World War.(SH, p.55) He likens his workers to a phantom army: 'He was gripped then by the sentiment of the old days of war and remembered the endless files of Scottish men he had seen come and go, rough, cheerful, fatalistic, endlessly and blindly suffering'. (SH, p.55) However Leslie's sentimental worry over the situation is no good to his workers, and its unconvincing representation can be regarded as a flaw in Blake's text.

The demoralisation of unemployment is represented in *No Mean City*. Even though crime does pay better than work for the protagonist Johnnie Stark who, 'knew that one well-organised raid might bring him in more money than two months of solid work',(NMC, p.182) he too eventually becomes negatively infected by the ennui of unemployment, 'fed up with life...that frustration of the spirit which comes at times to every healthy unemployed man'.(NMC, p.296) Years of unemployment gradually wear down Johnnie's will, hope and aspirations: 'Unemployment, which he had made no serious effort to escape, had, nevertheless, lowered his morale. It always does and always must do. Glasgow, the second city in the Empire, with a third of its adult population idle, bears tragic witness to this indisputable fact.' (NMC, p.255) The effects of extended unemployment on the huddled groups of men who hung about the street corners of 1930s Glasgow are documented by Muir in *Scottish Journey*, in an impressionistic description of the previously industrious and busy shipbuilding quarter of Clydeside, where now the workers have been deprived not only of their means of existence, but also of their very voice and vitality:

The very air seems empty around them, as if it had been drained of some essential property; they scarcely talk, what they say seems

---

29 David Kirkwood, *My Life of Revolt* (George.G. Harrap: London, 1935), p.251.

hardly to break the silence ... there is hardly anything but this silence, which one would take to be the silence of a dead town if it were not for the numberless empty-looking groups of unemployed men standing about the pavements.[30]

From the outset *Gael Over Glasgow* documents the difficulty of finding work when so many were unemployed: 'Too many good men haven't got their jobs back after the war'. (GG, p.17) The demoralisation of unemployment is illustrated: 'years of this demeaning process destroy pride and nobility...driving the shame and bitterness deep into a man's soul' (GG, p.224). After weeks of tramping up and down the industrial Clyde searching for work Brian feels hopeless: 'The Labour Exchanges were crowded with men signing the unemployed register and long queues of men stretched down the streets; ... clerks had smiled cynically and added his name to the hundreds of engineers who had visited the office before him'. (GG, p.233) *Gael Over Glasgow* also expresses the frustration of dealing with officialdom and bureaucracy in the emergent and inadequate British welfare system at the time:

> they were called before committees of apparently intelligent officials, who gravely examined and cross-questioned them to see if they were looking for work or not. If you were a fool and took this insulting farce seriously and told them the truth they stopped your dole for not looking for a thing that did not exist – a job. (GG, p.234)

Muir describes with great pathos what he labels, 'the everlasting Sunday Land of the unemployed';[31] the waste of human talent and resulting existential sense of emptiness. Although there is no longer semi-starvation, much of Muir's critique continues to be applicable today with the continuing high unemployment in Glasgow over seventy years later.

> At forty, at thirty, at twenty, sometimes at birth, they are pensioned off from civilisation, and their lives consigned to inactivity and ennui ... The enforced inactivity, the loss of manual skill, the perpetual scrimping to keep alive, the slow eating away of dignity and independence, the compulsory spectacle of semi-starvation around one, in the faces of the children one has brought into the world.[32]

30 Edwin Muir, *Scottish Journey*, p.138.
31 Muir, *Scottish Journey*, p.142.
32 Ibid, pp.143-144

The Buroo and The Dole

By 1933 over 30% of the Glasgow work-force was dependent on social security or 'poor relief', as opposed to 25% for the rest of Scotland.[33] The high levels of unemployment in the inter-war period had a devastating effect on the standard of living of the poorest families. Many came to rely on the state social security system known as 'the dole' to provide their means of subsistence. This is well documented in all five of the Glasgow realist novels.

Unemployment benefit in the 1930s is delineated in *Major Operation*: 'Two parents and two children. Twenty-nine shillings for the lot...Ten shillings for rent. That leaves nineteen for food....and nothing for fire or light or clothes or a newspaper or a night at the pictures. Nothing for illness, trouble and unforeseen circumstances'. (MO, p.380) Muir made a real attempt to understand the ramifications of unemployment, given that it made up such a significant part of the socio-economic milieu of his time. In an ironic indictment of the social security system, he argues that while Industrialism had changed the attitude to the poor insofar as to create a social conscience on the part of the wealthy, he calculated that the dole of the time did not provide more than a basic subsistence to prevent the unemployed from dying of starvation.[34]

In *The Shipbuilders* Danny eventually realises that, 'There was no real work going on Clydeside. Up and down the River the yards lay empty... It was bad, hundreds, thousands, of his mates on the Dole or the Parish'. (SH, p.86) The dole office is referred to in the novels as 'the Buroo' — from 'Bureau', which pre-dated emergence of the British Welfare State after the Second World War. The term is still used colloquially in Glasgow today, although the official name has changed over the years during the process of transforming poor relief into social security.[35] The history of social welfare in Britain evolved from 1911 with the introduction of limited unemployment insurance administered by the Labour Exchange, available for a specified time after the loss of a job. When this unemployment benefit was exhausted for a particular worker, then the next stage was to apply for Parish Relief, known simply in the novels as 'The

---

33 Maver, *Glasgow*, p.205
34   Edwin Muir, *Scottish Journey*, p.134.
35   A process described by C.de B.Murray, *How Scotland is Governed*. (Moray Press: Edinburgh, 1938).

Parish'. The much hated Means Test introduced in Britain in 1931 assessed the income and assets of all the members of a family together, thus reducing the benefit. David Stenhouse, the Glasgow Town Clerk in 1933, describes how the process was administered by the Glasgow Corporation under the supervision of the Director of Public Assistance.[36] Protests against the Means Test are documented in the novels, and the logistics of the system described in *Gael Over Glasgow*: 'the Means Test decreed that Brian was not entitled to any money as his father's wages spread over all three just touched the pauper's scale.' (GG, p, 309)

The five novels all convey a sense that the shame of the dole queue was the worst disgrace for the Glasgow worker. Although this does not apply to the work-shy Johnnie Stark and his gang in *No Mean City*; unemployment eventually depresses even him. On his return to working as a coalman after a long period of idleness he is so happy that, 'He seldom bothered to think that there was barely twelve shillings difference between his wages for a hard week's work and the money he could draw from "the buroo" for nothing'. (NMC, p.122) In due course however, it does occur to Johnny 'that he was slaving like a navvy for next to nothing a week. He knew that if he were sacked he would go "on the dole" to draw, as of right – for he was an insured worker – almost two thirds of his actual salary'. (NMC, p.183) So Johnnie gives up his coalman job to return to idleness.

A fear of the demoralisation of unemployment pervades *The Shipbuilders*: 'No worker on Clydeside could do anything but fear that this infection of unemployment would touch him yet.' Danny the riveter understands how 'even Pagan's may one day be as a score of yards up and down the river – empty, silent, while the men slouched about street corners outside and queued up automatically at the Buroo. That last offence to decency and pride'. (SH, p.17) And again later in the novel, 'to be a dole-drawer, to queue up with the workshies and the halflins at the Buroo, that last humiliation of his artisan pride'. (SH, p.129) When eventually Danny is forced to go on the dole: 'He registered at the Buroo. He stood in queues with others like him. He hung about street corners, hands in pockets, staring emptily at passing trams ...There were hundreds of thousands in the sinking ship with him'. (SH, p.137) However unlike the unemployed protagonists in the other novels, Danny does not join a union or

---

36 David Stenhouse, *Glasgow: Its Municipal Undertakings and Enterprise.* (Glasgow Corporation: Glasgow, 1933) p. 116.

go on hunger marches. Despite the descriptions of deprivation in *The Shipbuilders*, nowhere in the narrative does this translate into political action.

The sense of humiliation at being without work is also documented in *Hunger March*. Struggling to define his own identity as an unemployed worker, Joe asks himself if he is indeed what others have labelled him, 'A moocher? A supporter of the buroo?' (HM, p.76) And it is an uneasy and angry irony that is conveyed through the voice of Jimmy the journalist in *Hunger March* when deconstructing the dole and the attitude of the bourgeoisie towards the unemployed: 'In this Christian country of ours, none need starve ... Not so long as he had strength to drag himself out to draw his dole. On it he could live like a lord on a diet for obesity'. (HM, pp.160-161).

There is also ironic satirising in *Major Operation* of the bourgeois attitude towards working class unemployment and the social security system. This is articulated in the novel as the collective voice of the generic middle class which Barke holds up for critical consideration: 'It's this damned dole that's at the bottom of the trouble....Unemployment they call it: but it's just laziness. Work-shys. Never have worked and never will work. But do they go without? When the dole's exhausted they go to Public Assistance: they're made for life then'. (MO, p.376) And George's own viewpoint towards an unemployed demonstration, before his bankruptcy in *Major Operation*, is one of intolerant irritation: 'Unemployed becoming a menace, silly of them demonstrating during business hours.... Hadn't they got the dole? Want jam on it. Sapping morale. Terrific burden on country.' (MO, p.128)

Both Muir and Grassic Gibbon view the commercial essence of Glasgow as irredeemably negative. With reference to the brutal consequences of capitalism, Gibbon asks in *Scottish Scene*, 'Why did men ever allow themselves to become enslaved to a thing so obscene and so foul...?'[37] He denounces the quality of life for the Glasgow unemployed: 'doomed to long days of staring vacuity, of shoelessness, of shivering hidings in this and that mean runway when the landlords' agents come, of mean and desperate begging at Labour Exchanges and Public Assistance Committees'.[38]

---

37 Lewis Grassic Gibbon and Hugh MacDiarmid, *Scottish Scene*, p.137.
38 Ibid. p.138.

Conclusion

The response of Capitalism to the inter-war depression and to subsequent economic slumps was to rationalise and relocate its resources. Survival of the system is the primary goal even at the expense of jettisoning the livelihoods of those deemed inefficient. Glasgow's very success in the field of heavy industry meant it was vulnerable to this reallocation of resources, and the events within the novels reflect this. Shipbuilding may not have been the major industry, but so many other industries were interdependent with it that when the shipyards caught a cold, the rest of Clydeside sneezed. The depression caused unemployment and an exodus from the region by those in search of work. Perhaps the very pride with which the Second City regarded its achievements worked as hubris. Possibly this is best reflected in the transformation of George's opinion of the casualties of commerce in *Major Operation*. All the novels are informed by, and arise from the economic turmoil of the times. They are not only written in ink but with the haemorrhaging life-blood of Glasgow's industries. The sheer magnitude of the vulnerable heavy-industries meant the entire local economy was in crisis, with the concomitant collateral damage on all who dwelt there.

There were only two major shipyards operating in 2010 on the Upper Clyde: both run by BAE Systems but known by many of their workers by their old names: BAE Govan as Fairfield's and BAE Scotstoun as Yarrows. Some of the current workers are veteran survivors of the last shipyards that closed in the 1970s, and they are carriers of the skills and the oral history of the shipyards. The old Fairfield's administration offices were recently reclaimed for renovation by the local community, and now echo once again to the sound of pounding metal in the BAE shipyard next door, busy at the time of writing with contracts for destroyers and aircraft carriers for the Royal Navy, that it is hoped are not cancelled due to the recent economic downturn and government cutbacks in 2009. The pride and legacy of the shipyards still loom large in the popular consciousness of Glaswegians, and the history of the craftsmanship is on display in the Glasgow Transport museum.

Ironies and paradoxes abound in the history of Glasgow. It is ironic that the city grew around a place where the Clyde was shallow enough to ford, and that a city on a river too shallow for large ships should subsequently have become the greatest iconic shipbuilding city of its time. It is also ironic that Glasgow, the great commercial city based on mercantile capital initially gained through profit from Atlantic trade with the colonies, should have also become known as one of the great working class Socialist cities of the United Kingdom; and that now it should look back with nostalgia to a past glory based on the accumulation of wealth for the bourgeoisie, created through exploitation of the working class.

3   City as Protagonist

Realistic Representations of Inter-war Glasgow

Introduction

The most interesting aspect of the five Glasgow novels — *Hunger March* (1934) by Dot Allan, *Major Operation* (1936) by James Barke, *The Shipbuilders* (1935) by George Blake, *No Mean City* (1935) by Alexander McArthur and H. Kingsley Long, and *Gael Over Glasgow* (1937) by Edward Shiels — may be their realistic representation of the city and its social realities during the inter-war era. The novels all feature Glasgow as protagonist – the city as central character, describing it at a particular moment, fixing it for posterity in the literary imagination. This chapter examines how realistically the representations and tropes used to signify the city in the novels correspond to contemporary non-fictional depictions of social conditions in Glasgow at the time.

The five novels can be regarded as an expression of an urban literary genre that emerged in Scotland during the inter-war era. The intention of this nascent realistic genre was to reveal the gritty truth of the city and thereby counteract the dominant bucolic, rural trend in Scottish literature known as Kailyard. The novels are also a rejection of the so-called Urban Kailyard that had previously glossed over the negative aspects of the city, and they appear determined to reveal its sordid underbelly.[1] The prevailing imagery of the realistic inter-war novels is that of the corrupting city: highlighting social conditions of poverty, degradation, alcohol, crime, and gang violence. There is the repeated metaphor of the corrosive influence of the slums, and the people who become like the slums. What all the novels examined here have in common is that inter-war Glasgow functions not only as setting, but also as protagonist. The city is an entity which has a life and existence of its own, apart from the narrative and the life of the characters. The city as entity exists as a discrete unit. The character of the city is not always positive, but dark, degenerate, corrupt, monstrous. Its reeking slums represent a Dionysian embodiment of the shadow-side of capitalism, placed in ironic juxtaposition

---

1   See discussion of the Kailyard in Chapter One.

with the Apollonian eclecticism of its architecture and temples to commercialism. The characters in the novels struggle for meaning in the streets, houses and work places (if they are lucky enough to have a job and a house) of an economically and culturally impoverished Glasgow, often succumbing to alcohol and violence, but the city continues.

Nonetheless, Glaswegians knew how to enjoy themselves despite their hard environment. Drink was a central theme and the city was known as dancing mad. The people were also internationally famous for their particular form of language and humour. The 'Glasgow patter' is legendary: a guttural, nasal speech uttered at a speed that has newcomers imagining it to be a language other than English. Lewis Grassic Gibbon describes the Glasgow dialect as 'a herd-beast delighting in vocal discordance and orgiastic aural abandon'.[2] Glaswegians also excel at insulting each other, and a tradition peculiar to the city is known as 'sherricking'[3], or the public humiliation of someone who is 'getting above themselves', described in its full glorious manifestation in several passages of *No Mean City*. In what may be regarded as a form of inverse snobbery, Glaswegians take perverse pride in their proletarian roots and in debunking any suspected class pretension. 'Humane irreverence' is Glasgow's greatest export according to William McIlvanney, who explains that the essence of Glasgow speech is a deflation of pomposity:

> Those who are for me the truest Glaswegians, the inheritors of the tradition, the keepers of the faith, are terrible insisters that you don't lose touch for a second with your common humanity, that you don't get above yourself. They refuse to be intimidated by professional stature or reputation or attitude or name. But they can put you down with a style that almost constitutes a kindness.[4]

Grassic Gibbon understood the notion of city as character, and of the character of Glasgow as being distinct from that of Edinburgh or Aberdeen. His surreal metaphoric snapshots of cities in *Scottish Scene* read like newsreels, but for him Glasgow defies definition: 'no Scottish image of personification may display, even distortedly, the

---

2   Lewis Grassic Gibbon 'Glasgow' in *A Scots Hairst*, (Hutchinson: London, 1967:1978), p.85. First published in 1934 in *Scottish Scene*.
3   There are different spellings available for this
4   William McIlvanney, *Surviving the Shipwreck*, (Mainstream Publishing: Edinburgh, 1991) p.183.

essential Glasgow'.[5] Although it is difficult to define the essence of anything, it is possible to argue that the five novels examined here do succeed in realistically representing the character of the city and the city as character in some of its varying complexity, in a way that they do not always succeed in portraying the complexity of individual characters.

Mapping the City

The five novels examined here are all specifically set in Glasgow, and contain topographical descriptions of place reinforcing that this is Glasgow and not some other city. The mapping of a city is possible by examining its representations in realist literature. As culture derives from a combination of people and place, so the mapping of the city supports the location of the action and makes evident the social effect the city has upon its inhabitants.

Residential, industrial and commercial areas were all intermingled in inter-war Glasgow. Miles Horsey provides an instructive comparison:

> To a present-day observer, the abiding impression throughout the whole conurbation would have been one of close-packed population density and juxtaposition of housing and industry, as still found in Oriental cities such as Calcutta or Seoul.[6]

In the novels there is an acknowledgement of the conflicting and contradictory worlds of the city, in close cohabitation with each other. In *Gael Over Glasgow* the contrasts are overtly invoked:

> of disgusting slums and modern housing schemes; of hooligans living and mingling alongside intelligent workmen, of full blooded modernism brawling alongside Calvinism; of materialism and Catholicism all weaving and intertwining in that puzzling pattern of Society known as Clydeside.(GG, p.193)

Edwin Muir too maps Glasgow topography of the time — the working class residential areas in close proximity to the industrial

---

5   Lewis Grassic Gibbon,'Glasgow', *A Scots Hairst.* p.82.
6   Miles Horsey, *Tenements and Towers: Glasgow Working class Housing, 1890-1990.* (Royal Commission on the Ancient and Historical Monuments of Scotland 1990),p.2.

work places — reflecting the class stratification between the different areas: 'The slums in a Scottish industrial town are generally to be found either near the factories or in the oldest and most dilapidated of the tenements ... the tenements near the shipyards have mostly a clean and orderly look.'[7]

The narrative of the novels is located in what was at the time the working class mixed residential/industrial/shipyard districts. These were the Gorbals and Govan on the South Side of the Clyde, Partick on the North Side, and Clydebank some distance west of the city. Locations also include the middle class residential West End district surrounding the University of Glasgow; as well as the central business district of Glasgow around George Square. The Gorbals functions as a protagonist in its own right in *No Mean City*, a poor working class area of run down tenements identified in the novel as a 'slum'.[8] George Square in the City Centre and Glasgow Green in the East End had always been the central gathering places for civic protest, political demonstrations and marches (and still are to this day), a fact that is reflected in the novels. For example, the hunger marchers are portrayed in *Hunger March* and *Major Operation* as gathering in George Square: 'The Square was filled to overflowing. Demonstrators filled every approach. The centre of the Square was solid with sympathisers'. (MO, p.485) Glasgow Green, a traditional working class area of the city, was also a favourite setting for gang fights. After one such 'rammie' in *No Mean City*, Johnnie escapes by running towards Glasgow town centre, and the narrative mapping his escape route corresponds to areas and streets in the city that are still recognisable in 2009.

The descriptions of the streets of Glasgow on a Saturday night in the 1930s, when compared with today, indicate that the rhythms of the city have not changed much since the inter-war years despite the increase of motorised traffic. A chapter in *Major Operation* entitled 'The Pavement Patrol', describes the sociability of the city streets, and the desire of Glaswegians to publicly promenade — a habit which would have originated as an attempt to escape from overcrowded

7   Edwin Muir, *Scottish Journey* (Mainstream Publishing Company: Edinburgh, 1935:1979) p.125.

8   For discussion of the geographical history of the Gorbals see J.G. Robb. 'Suburb and Slum in Gorbals: Social and Residential Change 1800-1900.' in George Gordon and Brian Dicks (eds), *Scottish Urban History*. (Aberdeen University Press: Aberdeen, 1983), pp.132-135.

housing conditions. Sydney Checkland remarks on the different quality of Glasgow street life from other cities in Britain at the time:

> The very compression and density of the central part of Glasgow made for a city life that was colourful and lively. Instead of, as in many English cities, dying when the day's business was done, it was a place of human contact.[9]

Major Operation appears to be articulating two dissimilar ideas about class and the streets of Glasgow. There is the egalitarian ethos of all Glaswegians enjoying themselves together, walking the streets is free and open to all, both rich or poor, and the streets level class differences: 'Over the entire City the object of the (pavement) patrol was the same: there was an identity of interests between the middle class and the working class: the desire to be in the stream of life.' (MO, p.85) But a few lines later the narrative contradicts itself by suggesting that the streets also delineate class difference:

> The crowd in Sauchiehall Street was a middle class crowd: the crowd in Argyle Street was a working class crowd. In Dumbarton Road the crowd was more finely divided. On the north side paraded the better working class. On the south side the slum dwellers. (MO, p.85)

In the novels the city is sometimes taken apart and pieced together in a cubist collage of impressionist imagery, as in this passage from *The Shipbuilders*:

> The glazed wen of the People's Palace, the turgid Clyde, great buses, blue and red, passing over the bridge into the Gorbals – queer Jewish signs over doorways there – meaningless interminable streets of tenement houses, a horde of idle men at Bridgeton Cross, the evening papers with the racing results close to their eyes. (SH, p.148)

In both *The Shipbuilders* and *Gael Over Glasgow*, the regular tolling of the University of Glasgow clock is a constant reminder of the temporal nature of existence, a leitmotif throughout both narratives. The sound of the clock and the sight of the looming clock tower with its neo-Gothic crown of thorns is a familiar one in Glasgow, one which would have chimed with all the local readers of the books, so

---

9   Sydney Checkland, *The Upas Tree: Glasgow 1875-1975* (University of Glasgow Press: Glasgow, 1977), p.24.

functioning as an iconic landmark. The interesting anomaly about this clock is that to this day it has never possessed a clock face. The symbolism of a faceless clock, marking the temporal by chiming the time, but never spatially marked by possessing its own facade; perhaps an obscure metaphor for Glasgow's own identity, a blank countenance that catches all projections!

Housing and Slums

A preoccupation with the problem of the slums is evident in the journalism of the 1920s and 1930s. George Malcolm Thomson asserted in 1927, with a fear of contamination customary for the time, that: 'Half Scotland is slum-poisoned. The taint of the slum is in the nation's blood'.[10] Clydeside in particular had become, with the advent of the Industrial Revolution, the economic engine of Scotland. During this process the Glasgow urban proletariat were subject to the usual deprivations inherent in early capitalist development, but arguably in a more extreme form than many such cities in the United Kingdom. By the inter-war era the region was, 'Narrow and ugly, slum-cluttered, Scotland's industrial belt stretched tight across the 24 miles from the estuary of the Clyde to the Firth of Forth'.[11]

Inner-city overcrowding was a well known feature of nineteenth and early twentieth-century industrialised cities throughout the United Kingdom, but housing conditions in Glasgow were possibly more untenable than others. John Wheatley was one of the Red Clydesiders who publicised Glasgow's grim housing situation. He drew attention to the fact that by 1912 Glasgow was the most congested city in the in the United Kingdom, with a population density of 53 people per acre, as compared with 45 people per acre for Liverpool, the nearest city in terms of congestion.[12] *No Mean City* contains explicit descriptions of the housing shortage in Glasgow in the 1920s, and how life for tenants in the city was a weekly struggle to find the rent for the Factor, who wielded absolute power as the agent and manager appointed by a usually absent landlord: 'In 1924 overcrowding was such that any empty apartment was immediately re-let. The Factor

10 George M. Thomson, *Caledonia,Or the Future of the Scots* (Kegan Paul: London, 1927) p.21.

11 Michael Grieve in *Whither Scotland?*, ed. by D. Glen, (London: Gollancz, 1971) p.39.

12 John Wheatley, *Eight-Pound Cottages for Glasgow Citizens* (Glasgow Labour Party: Glasgow, 1913), p.10.

could pick and choose his tenants if he had a mind to'. (NMC, p.123) Apparently not much had changed since Glasgow was famously cited as an example of the worst housing conditions in Europe by Jellinger C. Symons, whose comments were influential on Fredrick Engels and quoted in his classic critique of capitalist society and the social effects of the Industrial Revolution – *The Condition of the Working Class in England*. Symons describes the Glasgow slums thus:

> this tangle of crime, filth and pestilence in the centre of the second city of the kingdom. An extended examination of the lowest districts of other cities never revealed anything half so bad, either in intensity of moral and physical infection, or in comparative density of population.[13]

Residential areas in Glasgow were dominated by four-storey sandstone tenements during the inter-war period. Built during the nineteenth century to accommodate a wide range of social classes, tenements appear to be egalitarian from the outside. However, as described in *No Mean City*, middle class tenements could contain many spacious rooms, while working class tenements would house large families in a one-room ('single end') or two-room ('room and kitchen') apartment. Tenements provided, and still do, an unmistakeable, iconic image of Glasgow, although Frank Worsdall points out that tenements became negatively associated with slums during the inter-war period, leading to their large scale demolition later in the twentieth century.[14]

In the preface of *No Mean City* the writers' stated project is to expose the poverty and untenable living conditions prevalent in Glasgow during the first decades of the twentieth century. Of the five inter-war novels this one provides the most graphic depictions of tenement life, enhancing its interest as a historical record. It contains descriptions of how sleeping in shared recessed 'hole-in-the-wall' cavity beds was a common feature of Glasgow housing at the time: 'windowless closets', 'little tombs about five feet by five by three and a half', (NMC, p.7) although the building of these recessed beds — labelled as 'cubicles of consumption' — had been outlawed

13 Jellinger .C.Symons, (1839) 'Reports from the Assistant Handloom Weavers Commissioners', cited in Fredrick Engels, *The Condition of the Working Class in England* published 1845 (Penguin: London,1987), p.79-80.

14 Frank Worsdall, *The Tenement, A Way of Life: A Social, Historical and Architectural Study of Housing in Glasgow.* (Chambers: Edinburgh, 1979),p.ix.

in 1913.[15] Few tenements had indoor plumbing, though by the end of the nineteenth century some of them were built with toilets — known colloquially as 'cludgies' — located on the half landing, and shared by families on two floors. The Royal Commission on Housing Report 1917 states that 93% of one room houses in Glasgow at the time had no inside toilet.[16] In *No Mean City* to possess an indoor bathroom becomes the highest housing aspiration (NMC, p.160), and the first marital home of Johnnie and Lizzie is described thus:

> The one room of Razor King's new home was tolerable "large"... Of course, it had no lavatory and there was no bathroom in the whole of the long, grey, four-storied tenement, nor, for that matter, in the whole of Crown Street. (NMC, p.123)

Working class living conditions in the novels can be verified by comparisons with texts such as *Up Oor Close* and *She Was Aye Workin'*, collections of working class oral narratives from Glasgow and Edinburgh spanning the 1900s-1960s. A prevailing memory from people who lived in tenements was that their mothers never stopped working. Life for tenement women was an endless cycle of cooking, cleaning and washing. Most families lived in houses of one or two rooms, so a great amount of time and effort was spent just packing away the beds in the morning to make room to move: 'The labour expended in keeping a one-room house in order is out of all proportion to its size. It is a constant succession of lifting, folding and hanging up, and if this relaxed for even a short time the confusion is overwhelming'.[17] This corroborates the opinion in *Gael Over Glasgow* that: 'it was impossible to keep these places tidy'. (GG, p.197) This novel also describes the negative effect of the hard living conditions on the women of the Glasgow tenements:

> One could hardly imagine those sad, dull eyed women one saw standing at the closes, telling their children fairy tales. Life was too cruel and hard here for them to indulge in imaginative flight. Reality, stark ugly realities were too close and insistent. (GG, p.198)

---

15 Helen Clark and Elizabeth Carnegie, *She was Aye Workin': Memories of Tenement Women in Edinburgh and Glasgow* (White Cockade: Oxford, 2003), p.17
16 Clark & Carnegie, p.18.
17 Mary Laird, Women's Labour League giving evidence to the Royal Commission on Housing 1913 in Clark and Carnegie *She was Aye Workin'*. p.107.

A Glasgow Councillor, who grew up in the city during the inter-war period, eulogises his mother and women like her:

> She died of overwork as many women did. The women of the working class in those days were first up in the morning and the last to go to bed. They kept the houses clean and they kept themselves clean, they kept the family's clothes clean in the worst possible conditions.[18]

Also paying tribute to 'those heroic women', David Kirkwood the Red Clydeside leader and Labour politician, describes the effect of unemployment on the working class women of Glasgow who had:

> seen their men depressed and nervous. They had long eaten up their little savings. They had struggled with untold splendour of sacrifice to pay the rent, to keep the husband and the children fed and clad; aye, and still more to keep up the spirit of their men.[19]

The material poverty of Glasgow tenement life forced women to work together. In *Hunger March* working class Mrs Humphry's feels a duty of care towards her neighbours in a way that middle class Mrs MacGregor, for whom she works, does not: 'It was queer but being under the same roof knit you all together whether you willed it or not. You were responsible for one another here.' (HM, p. 212)

The social organisation of women in Glasgow working class tenements is examined by Seán Damer in *Glasgow-Going for a Song* (1990), illustrating how living in close proximity to neighbours and sharing the washhouse and the stair-head toilets enforced the need for women to co-operate, and created a particular moral order. It was other women who made survival possible in extreme deprivation, through mutual support. Damer posits that there were two distinct working class cultures in Glasgow: that of men and that of women, and 'It was women who produced and reproduced the culture of the tenements', in what he refers to as a, 'sisterly, supportive series of densely impacted social networks – usually glossed over as "community spirit"'.[20]

Muir argues, much as Symons, quoted by Engels, had a century earlier, that the majority of the population of Glasgow during the

---

18 Clark and Carnegie, Ibid. p.13.
19 David Kirkwood, *My Life of Revolt*, (George.G. Harrap: London, 1935), p.252.
20 Seán Damer, *Glasgow — Going for a Song* (Lawrence & Wishart Ltd: London,1990), p.90.

inter-war era lived in some form of poverty caused by the competitive, capitalist economic system; that the slums 'penetrate the lives of all classes in Glasgow'.[21]   Muir's preferred themes in *Scottish Journey* and in much of his other work are: the impoverishment by industrialisation of human economic, social, and imaginative life; the urban wasteland; the resulting alienation from neighbours; and the anaesthetising of the senses in an untenable environment. On first arriving in Glasgow Muir was apparently traumatised by the daily walk to his workplace on the South side of Glasgow through the slums of the Gorbals: 'all the main thoroughfares leading from the town to the South Side were slums or semi-slums'.[22] This childhood revulsion towards urban squalor is to Muir, what the blacking factory was to Dickens, a strange mix of muse and obsession that appears in a creative crossover between his fiction and non-fiction. (In fact Muir also had a stint at working in a bone factory – a nadir of horror in his life.) It is particularly obvious in the chapter in his *Autobiography* entitled 'Glasgow', which mirrors the chapter of the same name in *Scottish Journey*, and explains the fixation with Eglinton Street in the Gorbals that emerges so strongly in his novel *Poor Tom*. Disgust at the industrial degradation of the city permeates these texts:

> These journeys filled me with a sense of degradation: the crumbling houses, the twisted faces, the obscene words casually heard in passing, the ancient, haunting stench of pollution and decay, the arrogant women, the mean men, the terrible children, daunted me.[23]

Oddly enough, Muir protests that he has never been tempted to actually investigate the slums of Glasgow, professing he has no wish to 'enter into competition with the narrators of horrors of this kind'. Nevertheless *Scottish Journey* evinces a scatological fascination with narrating the more nauseating aspects of slum housing, apparently in an attempt to shock his middle class readership from their complacency. Muir's visceral descriptions of slum living conditions can assume the speech cadences of an evangelical preacher:

> I have been told of slum courts so narrow that the refuse flung into them mounted and mounted in the course of years until it blocked

21 Muir, *Scottish Journey*, p.123.
22 Muir, Ibid, p.113.
23 Edwin Muir, *An Autobiography* (Canongate Classics: Edinburgh, 1954:1993), p.83.

all the house windows up to the second-top storey … and I have been given an idea of the stench rising from this rotting, half liquid mass.[24]

Lewis Grassic Gibbon, in *Scottish Scene*, employs similarly sordid imagery to describe poor housing conditions in Glasgow, his stated aim also being to shock his middle class reader (addressed to readers from 'Kelvinside' a bourgeois residential district in Glasgow) into an awareness of the dispossession of the city's underclass:

> In Glasgow there are over a hundred and fifty thousand human beings … living five or six to the single room … part of some great sloven of a tenement … its windows grimed with the unceasing wash and drift of coal-dust, its stairs narrow and befouled and steep … (who) eat and sleep and copulate and conceive and crawl into childhood in those waste jungles of stench and disease and hopelessness.[25]

An even more harrowing account of Glasgow slum conditions is given by David Kirkwood of his time at the bar, pleading the cause of Glasgow tenants at the Summary Ejectment Court of the Sheriffdom of Lanarkshire. This experience was a revelation for him, 'of the appalling misery in which thousands have to live, and a standing challenge to the system of society which makes such human misery possible.'[26] A substantiation of this sentiment is contained in Kirkwood's autobiography: 'No picture of rural poverty can compare with the grimy, sordid, diseased hideousness of life in a Glasgow slum, as it was in 1920'.[27]

City of Dreadful Night

The trope of the dark, corrupting, decadent influence of the city is sustained in all five inter-war novels. Glasgow is depicted as two worlds: the Apollonian -industrial, impersonal and imposing; contrasted with the Dionysian — human, emotional and sordid. It is not only steel which is consumed in the making of the leviathans of industry, but also flesh and blood, Glasgow's people. There are numerous examples painting a canvas of the city in binary oppositions. However this way of viewing the world can obscure

---

24 Muir, *Scottish Journey*, p.116.
25 Lewis Grassic Gibbon and Hugh MacDiarmid, *Scottish Scene* (Cedric Chivers: Bath, 1934:1974), p.137.
26 David Kirkwood *My Life of Revolt*, p175.
27 Kirkwood, Ibid. p.177.

the complexities inherent in everything. Glasgow is the sum of the integrated mixture of its parts. It is dark because it is also light, to see it as one or the other simplifies understanding. In *Gael Over Glasgow* the industrial workshops are overlooked by the sunny hills surrounding the dark city. In *Major Operation* and *Hunger March*, the sordid slums contrast with the wealthy commercial city centre. In *The Shipbuilders* the shipyards and their surrounding working class residential areas contrast with the houses of the bourgeoisie. In *No Mean City* the grubby Gorbals tenements contrast with the glittering dance-halls of the city.

Nature reflects culture in the five realist novels, frequently producing a parallel between the grey gloomy weather in Glasgow and depressed social conditions. Descriptions of the grey slate of the buildings, set against the grey rain, reflecting the grey sky, generating a peculiarly Glaswegian *mise-en-scène* in which everything works together to produce a homogenous grey, dark, wet, polluted whole, often indicative of, and contributing to, the misery of the protagonists in the literature.

Catherine Carswell believed that John Stuart Mill was wrong to find 'little else at Glasgow' except 'the stench of trade'. She argues in her autobiography *Lying Awake*, that there was much more in Glasgow; 'there was life, fierce and reckless and abundant, more especially when this life was low'.[28] Although Carswell is describing her years growing up in the city in the 1890s, social conditions had not changed much by the inter-war era judging from the images in *No Mean City*. Carswell's portrayal of the 'keelies',[29] or street children, 'those ragged, bare legged, blue footed, verminous and valgus children of Glasgow',[30] and the street crowd on a Saturday night, has the riotous vitality of Hogarth illustrating a London street a century earlier:

> where all the men and women, and even children at the breast, were openly drunk, drunkenness assumed an epic quality. It was an orgy, an abandon, a bacchanal, a celebration, a wild defiance. Shawled women fought, screaming and tearing out each other's hair, while the men stood round roaring them on with laughter. Other men and women reeled along in song or reclined oblivious in gutters.[31]

28 Catherine Carswell *Lying Awake*. (Canongate: Edinburgh, 1950:1997), p.18.
29 Carswell, Ibid. p.27.
30 Carswell, Ibid. p.16.
31 Carswell, Ibid. p.20.

Muir's first impression of Glaswegians, articulated in *Scottish Journey*, was that 'they were sad and incomprehensible distortions of nature', produced by the Glasgow environment which was 'barbarous and degrading':[32]

> these people seemed to have all passed through the slums, and to bear the knowledge of the slums within them. On their faces ... quite clearly displayed, a depraved and shameful knowledge, a knowledge which they could not have avoided acquiring.[33]

A chapter in *Major Operation* entitled 'Pain in the Second City' similarly delineates the effects of poverty on the working class of Glasgow:

> Men, women and children withered and wasted with disease. On infants, poverty, stupidity and ignorance bred a mountain mass of wailing pain and suffering. Malnutrition, rickets, consumption: the ravages of venereal disease: cruelly ignorant feeding: callous clothing: dirt: bed-bugs: lice, vermin. (MO, p.207)

Glasgow is presented as a visual spectacle in *Scottish Journey*, illustrating how the accumulated refuse in the streets of an industrial town reveal a primordial social soup, representing a synopsis of its collective existence:

> Scraps of newspaper, cigarette ends, rims of bowler hats, car tickets, orange peel, boot soles, chocolate paper, fish-and-chip paper, sixpences, broken bottles, pawn tickets and various human excretions: these several things, clean and dirty, liquid and solid, make up a sort of pudding or soup which is an image of the life of an industrial town. To this soup must be added an ubiquitous dry synthetic dust, the siftings of the factories, which is capable under rain of turning into a greasy paste resembling mud.[34]

Muir's observations above, echo Gibbon's olfactory description of the Gorbals in his essay entitled 'Glasgow': 'And out of the Gorbals arises again that foul breath as of a dying beast'.[35] Both sets of images evoke and endorse a chapter in *Major Operation* entitled 'the

---

32 Muir, *Scottish Journey*, p.114.
33 Muir, Ibid, pp.112-113.
34 Muir, Ibid, p.115.
35 Lewis Grassic Gibbon, 'Glasgow', in *A Scots Hairst*. (Hutchinson: London, 1967:1978), First published in 1934 in *Scottish Scene*. p.144.

Smells of Slumdom', which provides a similar sensory account of the disgusting details of slum life:

> The subway entrance breathed out its stale decayed air. Immediately beyond, where they turned into Walker Street, a warm odiferous waft of slumdom met them. It was not a smell that could be escaped. There were identifiable odours of cats' urine, decayed rubbish, infectious diseases, unwashed underclothing, intermingled with smells suggesting dry rot, unsanitary lavatories, overtaxed sewage pipes and the excrement of a billion bed-bugs. (MO, p.72)

The anthropomorphising trope of Glasgow giving birth to the gross, the monstrous, is one that recurs in the novels, and is also memorably and semi-humorously employed by Gibbon in his essay entitled 'Glasgow': 'The monster of Loch Ness is probably the lost soul of Glasgow, in scales and horns, disporting itself in the Highlands after evacuating finally and completely its mother-corpse'.[36] Later in this essay he extends the metaphor of death, degeneration and corruption: 'It may be a corpse, but the maggot-swarm upon it is fiercely alive'.[37] So likewise the grotesque city is evoked in *Major Operation*, where it is likened to a 'monstrous hermaphrodite' in labour, (MO, p.229) although it is not clear to what is being given birth. Is it something akin to Yeats' monstrous premonition, a rough beast of a new social order slouching towards Glasgow to be born at last? The metaphor for the power of a demonstrating crowd in *Hunger March* is: 'this mammoth specimen of the Atlantasaurus'. (HM, p.118) Whatever such a beast may be, there is a fear that something enormous and uncontainable is about to be born or break loose, the forces of chaos unleashed. Possibly it is ruling class paranoia at the prospect of profound revolutionary change that is revealed in a similar description of the hunger marchers in *Hunger March*:

> squalor embodied in the form of a dinosaurian monster before whose snapping jaws culture must vanish, frivolity must doff its tinsel, and in whose maw whole tracts of civilized country might conceivably disappear. … you felt if this shambling monster were held in bondage much longer it must stretch forth its great limbs, break loose and storm the buildings on either side. And for a space you saw Chaos rampant. You saw the outposts of civilized order tottering. (HM, pp.117-118)

36 Gibbon, Ibid. p.82.
37 Gibbon, Ibid. p.82.

Notwithstanding the negative portrayals of the city and its inhabitants, Glasgow does glint on occasion in the novels with the ability for enjoyment so characteristic of Glaswegians, seemingly irrepressible even in the depressed conditions of the inter-war period. The Glasgow music halls and dancing halls were famous and always packed: 'Glasgow was dancing mad between the wars and had many dancing halls such as the Locarno and the Clarendon … the largest was the Barrowland which could hold close to 2000 people'.[38] The Plaza opened at Eglinton Toll in 1922 (and existed until 1996) where, given its close proximity, folk from the Gorbals would have gathered for 'the jiggings'. The dancing tradition continued well into the twentieth century, as reported in *The Herald*: 'Glasgow was the dance capital of the UK in the 1950s and 1960s with 30 dance halls, a total unrivalled even by London'.[39] Along with the Glaswegian propensity for street promenading, the dancing was no doubt motivated by a desire to escape from overcrowded and difficult living conditions. There are glimpses of this vibrant social life in *The Shipbuilders* and *Gael Over Glasgow*, but it is most evident in *No Mean City*, where much of the action, both good and bad, takes place in the dance-halls. In this novel 'the dancing' is the place for young couples to meet, the nexus of social advancement for some, but also the scene of numerous gang fights. A dance hall manager from the period describes the reality of the scene: 'A lot of good people came into the Barrowland and a lot of bad people as well. I would say more good than bad because we had all the gangs from Bridgeton, the Gorbals and the Calton.'[40]

Crime was a convenient way of construing the corruption of the city, and gangs formed a vivid metaphor for journalists and novelists when describing the problems in Glasgow. Andrew Davies posits the influence of United States gangster movies on the interpretation of the gang phenomenon in the United Kingdom during the inter-war era. He reveals that the fear of the gang menace in the 1930s was fuelled by the press, in collusion with the police, who both responded to gang incidents with complex and often contradictory messages depending on their agenda. He argues that, 'Their rhetoric provided sensational copy. It was left to senior figures in the city's

---

38 Clark and Carnegie, *She was Aye Workin'*, p. 55.
39 Stephen Stewart 'Historians race to save pieces of the Plaza', *The Herald* , 5 July 2006.
40 Ibid.p.54.

press such as George Blake to ponder the consequences of Glasgow's notoriety for the city's prospects of economic recovery by the mid-1930s'.[41] Blake attempts to provide reasons for the gang culture in Glasgow in *The Shipbuilders*: 'Gangs of idle, unemployable boys, fed on American films and bad Sunday newspapers, seizing on so-called religious or sporting prejudices, arming themselves as they could, going about in bands, looking and hoping for trouble' (SH, p. 132). In the same novel, when Danny the Riveter's unemployed teenage son Peter is arrested for murder the father has, 'Some dim sense of the economic crime that had been committed against his son' and speculates that violence 'would never have been done or made by a boy who had worn himself out in a fitting shop or on the rusty deck of a ship in the making.' (SH, p.134)

The novels portray an ambivalent Glaswegian working class attitude towards the police, described somewhat patronisingly in *The Shipbuilders* as 'those aloof authoritarians his class at once feared and disliked and respected'. (SH, p.132) Cynicism toward the authorities permeates *No Mean City* where 'the polis' are presented as being, for the most part, ineffectual. Damer argues that gangs were the creation of unemployment and poverty, that *No Mean City* fails to get the gang phenomenon into perspective, and more contentiously, that 'the biggest and most successful gang in Glasgow was always the city's police force'.[42] From 1931 Glasgow's Chief Constable was Percy Sillitoe, a controversial figure who wrote his own personal interpretation of inter-war policing in *Cloak Without Dagger*.[43] Another economic rationale for gangs is offered in *Gael Over Glasgow*, 'Men instinctively shrank from these surroundings, and men drew closer to each other. Solitude meant madness in a place like this. Hence the groups huddled at the corners, hence the gangs.' (GG, p.128) The sense is that the empowerment of gang status functions as an antidote to the disempowerment of those who fail to flourish within the capitalist system.

Gang feuds function as a dark motif throughout *No Mean City* in which the desire to escape from the slums is one of the reasons advanced by the novel for the existence of the Glasgow gangs. The stated aim of the novel from the outset is to illustrate Glasgow's

---

41 Andrew Davies, 'The Scottish Chicago? From hooligans to gangsters in inter-war Glasgow'. *Cultural and Social History*, Vol 4, issue 4, 2007. p. 524.
42 Damer, Glasgow — *Going for a Song*. p.149.
43 Percy Sillitoe, *Cloak Without Dagger*,(Cassell & Co: London,1955)

claim to violence; which it argues is a result of the poverty and degradation of its citizens. The gangs are territorially based, with Johnnie's Gorbals' gang feuding against gangs from other working class districts in Glasgow — Plantation, Bridgeton and Townhead. At the height of his fame and power in the Gorbals, Johnnie Stark the Razor King can be assured that, 'there were at least five hundred young men in the district now ready and eager to face the armed strength of any other division in the city.' (NMC, p.147) Explicitly violent imagery periodically punctuates the text. There is much crashing-down of broken bottles on faces and kicking-in with iron-shod boots of heads: 'Fighting is truly one of the amusements of the tenements. Nearly all the young people join in, if not as fighters themselves, at least as spectators and cheering supporters', (NMC, p.44) and there is, 'that queer admiration for a champion gangster which exists in the slums even among people who have nothing to do with the gangs.'(NMC, p.123) The descriptions of Glasgow gang fights are fearfully graphic and realistic, and this pornography of violence must have added to the titillating appeal of the novel. One of the most explicit of these passages in *No Mean City* is described as an epic gang battle in Albion Street involving a crowd of more than two thousand 'slummies':

> the opposing mobs surged down it from opposite ends in a tumult of shouting and yelling and cursing and defiance. Stones and bottles were thrown from one crowd to the other before the front ranks met....Then, as the front rank hooligans joined battle, the high-pitched screams of the girls goaded them on until there were half a hundred furious fights in progress at once. The whole mob reeled and sprawled and swirled and eddied like a flooded river between narrow banks. (NMC, p. 180)

As Damer argues –'Nobody denies that Glasgow is a tough city and that its people ...are tough, but that toughness was a necessary and unwanted outcome of historically harsh working conditions and harsher living conditions.' [44]

---

44 Damer, Ibid.

Models of Masculinity

Glasgow evolved its own brand of machismo through a particularly harsh historical process. Working class male identity was moulded by the difficult and dangerous work in the shipyards and heavy industries of the city. Social conditions were often brutal and dehumanising. The 'Glasgow Hard Man' became a parody of entrapped masculinity: self-destructive, drunken and violent. But what were Glaswegian notions of masculinity during the inter-war era? What was accepted and expected of a man? Is this informed by, or in dialectical relationship with, portrayals of men in the realist novels, which could also have provided a model for male behavior at the time? Did novels like *No Mean City* encourage emulation in the way that Davies suggests Hollywood gangster movies of the era influenced British gang culture? Was there a unitary masculinity? There are inherent contradictions in the term. Ruling-class power had an intrinsic interest in young Scottish men flaunting their masculinity to feed the armies of Imperial Britain, and the warrior tradition is not noted for emotional depth and sensitivity. Skilled work created a strong symbol of potency and masculinity, but unemployment emasculated male identity and self esteem. So, did the development of the notion of the Glasgow hard man mask enormous complexity in the actual lives of Glaswegian working class men?

Hegemonic masculinity in the West of Scotland came to be associated solely with negative characteristics depicting men as unemotional, independent, non-nurturing, aggressive, and dispassionate, actually some of the causes of criminal behaviour. There are links between excessive alcohol consumption and the male role. The use of alcohol and a licence to overindulge are deeply rooted in expectations of male behaviour in Glasgow. It is difficult for men to abstain in a culture where not drinking is considered weak and feminine. Holding your drink without becoming intoxicated becomes an expression of male identity and gender affirmation. Male social constructs in the West of Scotland tend to focus around the hub of the pub. This culture evolved as a release from the overcrowded living conditions in working class homes, as illustrated in the novels. The pub could also be seen to function as a substitute for the institution of the Kirk: the place for social gathering with knots of people standing around on the street at closing time, much like the social groupings that form after a church service. But the social cohesion of pubs can transform into social division as illustrated in the novels: hard men, plus pub, plus alcohol, plus too much free time when unemployed, tends to add up to violence, neglect and abandonment of family responsibility, which in turn leads to guilt, feeding into lack of self-esteem, requiring more alcohol to ease the pain. Even gentle Danny in *The Shipbuilders* gets trapped into this cycle of self-destructive behaviour when he loses his job, takes to the drink, and has to restrain himself from hitting his annoying wife.

Violence has always been abundant in Glasgow, however it is documented that domestic violence towards women after the pubs had closed was far worse than any of the gang street battles.[45] In *No Mean City* most of the fathers and husbands depicted in the novel are unemployed, alcoholic, and habitually abusive towards their wives and children, contributing to an environment of domestic instability, terror and the reproduction of dysfunctional relationships. Johnnie's father John Stark is the archetype of the bad father. He takes no responsibility for his progeny, and 'wondered grimly how it was that all the women in the slums seemed to want kids' whom he regards as 'breadsnappers'. (NMC, p.10) He 'bashes' his wife and children, who live in constant fear of him but won't put him in jail; even after he fractures his wife's skull with a beer bottle she 'refuses to give evidence against her husband'. (NMC, p.31) There is also a conspiracy of silence from the neighbours. His son Johnnie is less relentlessly violent towards his women, but does not hesitate to give them a 'careless blow' now and again. He is not regarded as a 'woman-beater' because he only hits his pregnant ex-girlfriend Mary when she is 'sherricking'[46] him, and refrains from 'bashing' Lizzie his wife until several years into their marriage. (NMC, p.189) It is within this crucible of violence that Johnnie develops into the 'Razor King', afraid of nothing but ridicule, of 'being laughed at by the neighbours'. (NMC, p.27)

The Glasgow hard man model of masculinity contains similar characteristics to those popular in American movies of the first half of the twentieth century: Western cowboys and urban gangsters, epitomised by strength, boldness, being in control, meeting challenges in dangerous situations, and a cool toughness; along with

---

45 Irene Maver, *Glasgow* (Edinburgh University Press: Edinburgh, 2000), p.254.
46 A Glasgow ritual of public humiliation

risk-taking behaviours such as smoking, drinking, and gambling.[47] Mark McManus, the first actor to play Taggart the popular Glasgow detective in the television series of the same name, defines the ontological roots of the Glasgow 'hard man', with a pertinent observation regarding the ongoing reproduction of a culture of violence in the city:

> The hard man is ingrained in Glasgow history. He came to prominence in the "*No Mean City* Era" between the wars, a time of razor kings and mass gang fights, but his origins go back to the overcrowded slum housing of Glasgow's early Industrial period. Conditions have changed since then, although no-one in their right mind would claim that poverty and unemployment have been conquered. In today's city we still have unacceptable levels of domestic tension, depression and hopelessness. Some of its victims erupt into violence, others neglect family duties or just cannot cope with them, and this creates a new wave of urban casualties – their children.[48]

No Mean City was one of the first in a long genre of novels about Glasgow hard men and their exploits. It traces the evolution of its protagonist Johnnie Stark into the archetypical representation of the Glasgow hard man, gang leader, known as the 'Razor King' because of his weapons of choice, two cut-throat razors which he wields effectively in his many battles. The novel is a sociological study in the making of a type:

> Many a young gangster, not yet lost to all decent feeling, deliberately hardens his heart as he hardens his muscles. His vanity compels him to be brutal. There must be nothing soft about a 'razor king'. (NMC, p.52) The least faltering by the Razor King would have turned the spectators into a pack of wolves. (NMC, p.65)

Major Operation describes a shipyard work crew, in a passage that can only be regarded as a misguided attempt at irony, so shocking is its seeming affirmation of a violent and misogynistic male identity:

> They were raw but they were genuine – when you got to know them. They weren't angels of course. Razor slashers, wife beaters,

---

47 See discussion of Andrew Davies' work on the influence of American gangster movies earlier in this chapter.

48 Mark McManus & Glenn Chandler. *Taggart's Glasgow*. (Lennard Publishing: Oxford, 1989), p.148.

incestmongers, adulterers, drunkards, blackmailers, gangsters ... But
a man, morally rotten, didn't work long with MacKelvie. (MO, p.41)

Unemployment for men in a capitalist system can lead to
emasculation and low self esteem. Thus it is not too difficult to
imagine that the crisis of capitalism resulted in a crisis of confidence
in the collective male Glaswegian psyche during the inter-war era.
Compounding the economic disempowerment of unemployment,
the loss of the traditional breadwinner role within the family
unit would have been emotionally undermining. Shipyards and
engineering were the domain of men. (Women entered this world
during the world wars but men regained control soon after.) In *The
Shipbuilders*, Leslie is happiest when 'reestablished as the man of
action', whereas for Peter, Danny's older son, he 'becomes the big
man in the house on the strength of a job'. (SH, p.95) This connection
between work and self-esteem is evident in how Danny's masculine
pride preventing him from drawing social security payments when
he is made redundant from the shipyard. Male identity in the novels
is rooted in work, although this identity is a social construct and as
such hides the underlying reality. It is also possible that the menfolk
cannot deal with the reality of their alienated existence at any time,
but when preoccupied with work, can disguise this from themselves;
and when not working, can anaesthetize themselves from reality
with alcohol.

The notion of 'manliness' runs as a repeated refrain throughout
two of the novels. In *Gael Over Glasgow* there is an obsession with
'being manly' evident in Brian's mother's view of him, in his own
dreams of manhood, and finally, in his uncle's declaration on 'the State
of Scotland' and how it is 'a man's job to make it a nation'. (GG, p.353)
In *No Mean City* Lily constantly exhorts her boyfriend Bobby to be 'a
wee bit manly'. (NMC, p.163) The overarching tone of the narrrative
derides notions of manliness – then undercuts this by describing
Bobby as being unmanly. When he sensibly runs away from the final
fight in the novel, leaving Johnnie and Peter to battle it out alone,
the judgement of the narrative voice is that, 'Bobby was never very
manly'. (NMC, p.312) The numerous repetitions of the word 'manly'
in both novels naturalises the construct, and emphasises how its
absence leaves the main characters adrift.

But is there a unitary notion of masculinity expressed in the
Glasgow novels? What of the possibility of diverse masculinities?

There is not only one norm of the Glaswegian male, and some of the realistic novels do depict men who are different from the stereotype, men who are capable of sensitivity, gentleness and nurturing. Aside from representing the Glasgow hard man, the novels of the 1930s also show a softer side to Glaswegian men. Domestic economic arrangements in the novels unexpectedly subvert conventional notions of masculinity. For example in *The Shipbuilders* Danny's gender role perforce changes after he loses his job. When his wife leaves him he comes to dominate the domestic by default, as the housekeeper and primary carer of his son. Leslie in *The Shipbuilders* displays more nurturing affection for his son than does his wife, the cold-hearted Blanche. Jock in *Major Operation* nurtures his new friend George. Even uber-masculine Johnnie can cook his own supper as *No Mean City* helpfully explains: 'Most working class men can cook for themselves and the unemployed habitually do when their wives are lucky enough to be at the toil. They often look after the house and children too.' (NMC, p.208) This novel also reveals the general acceptance in working class Glasgow of the time that the woman is often the financial provider and manager in the household, 'a very normal state of affairs, as indeed it was, and still is in modern Glasgow.' (NMC, p.202) So there is a slippage towards anti-patrician values and characterisation. Men who are denied the opportunity to function within their designated social role can experience the upsurge of unaccustomed emotions. This could possibly contribute to a construction of the Glasgow 'soft man' – no doubt a problematic notion in the West of Scotland.

Conclusion

The city has been considered here as character, topography, housing, social interaction, violence, masculinity and crime. The way in which a city is put together materially incarnates certain social segregations and produces particular contradictions. For example, the historic juxtaposition of housing with the shipyards in Glasgow created working class solidarity, and simultaneously effected segregation from the middle classes. The city produced a certain mentality and persona which can be regarded as a 'spirit of Glasgow'. Deprivation can result in a shared camaraderie. Working class solidarity was a practical survival mechanism for those who possessed little, relying upon each other for support. The isolation from the middle classes would also serve to increase the cohesion of the working classes, strengthening the sense of belonging to a distinct group, creating pride in surviving through adversity, while developing a wry sense of humour as a coping mechanism. The drink too would function in this manner, while exaggerated toughness, particularly masculinity, would provide a social template for dealing with heavy blows such as the death of children and general ill-health. These characteristics can also be somewhat over-sentimentalised by the mostly middle class writers of the inter-war novels.

Realism in fiction can match and connect with historical data and help reconstruct reality; in the five novels studied here this is diagnostic rather than remedial. The Glasgow proletarian novels of the inter-war period tend to be infused with a deep existential pessimism, narrating the decline of the city and the demoralisation of the population caused by unemployment, but without offering solutions to the problems or a vision of a way out. Although crude and melodramatic in parts, most of the texts have a certain archetypal power. They serve to record the credible voices and lives of the people of Glasgow during the inter-war era that may otherwise have been lost to history. The novels provide an interesting insight into a once powerful Second City of the British Empire at a particular moment in its historical development, documenting the social conditions in Glasgow during the Great Depression, providing the reader with a realistic representation of the inter-war city.

4   Revolutionary City

Inter-war Politics and Red Clydeside

Introduction

The idea of Revolutionary Glasgow had its roots in a range of radical social reform movements in the city throughout the eighteenth and nineteenth centuries, reaching realisation during the first three decades of the twentieth century when Glasgow's popular image evolved into that of a militant proletarian city. The creation of this symbolism and the myths fostered thereby were both historical and literary: represented in the realistic novels of Clydeside and by the supporting evidence in non-fictional accounts of the era they describe, including those of the influential autobiographies of the political leaders from the time. The inter-war era was one of increasing empowerment and political action by the labour movement in Glasgow. It was a period when the city came to be associated with various stereotypes including Socialism, Communism, the Labour Movement, and Red Clydeside. This chapter enquires whether the economic crisis of the Great Depression, and the political phenomenon of Red Clydeside, created the necessary and sufficient conditions for a radical political revolution in Glasgow during the inter-war era; and if so, what evidence there is for this in the novels, as well as in contemporary and consequent political analyses.

During the first decades of the twentieth century there was increased global political consciousness as the international working class organised to struggle for a fair share of the profits they were generating. In Glasgow before 1914 there was already a committed, well-organised political infrastructure consisting of different Marxist and socialist groups. This grew rapidly with political action in the city during the First World War creating a radicalising effect on the labour movement. The anti-War Peace Movement and the Rent Strikes politicised the population of Clydeside, leading to a growth in the popularity of left-wing political parties such as the Independent Labour Party (ILP), the British Socialist Party (BSP), and the Socialist Labour Party (SLP). After the 1917 success of the Russian Revolution there was significantly increased political activity on the streets of

Glasgow. At the time Glasgow and central Scotland, 'was just about the most proletarianised area of the world … It also contained within it a complicated and potentially explosive mixture of political tensions'.[1] There was developing militancy in the workplace, and a new form of workers organisation, the Shop Stewards movement, formalised by the establishment of the Clyde Workers Committee. There also emerged a new form of political activism and organisation based in working class communities. It was in this context that the image of 'Red Clydeside' developed.

There is a long tradition of socialist organisations in Glasgow. The inter-war novels examined here all refer to this history, and reflect how the 1920s and 1930s resulted in increasing political and industrial unrest on Clydeside. This new militancy characterised an empowered, unionised workforce in constant conflict with the bosses to improve wages and working conditions. The industrialists in turn attempted to keep down the costs of labour and prevent further decreases in profits at a time when most of Glasgow's enterprise was struggling to stay in business. The novels also illustrate how, as the Great Depression advanced during the 1930s, the increasing numbers of unemployed workers also became increasingly militant and organised, although not always to great effect.

Red Clydeside and the Revolution – the Forty Hour Week Strike 1919

Radicalism on Clydeside during the first decades of the twentieth century was a product of the spontaneous reaction of the unemployed and working classes to the material conditions of their oppression; as well as leadership by a local vanguard of the Communist Party with close connections to Soviet Russia. Defining 'Red Clydeside' is complicated as it was not a coherent political movement and owed much of its swashbuckling status to the power of the British press. It could be said to represent the small parliamentary group more usually known as 'the Clydesiders', or the whole continuum of left-wing politics in and around Glasgow, including communists, anarchists and the Marxist-inclined Independent Labour Party (ILP).[2]

1 John Foster, 'Scotland and the Russian Revolution', *Scottish Labour History Society*, Vol. 23 1988 p.23.
2 It is not known exactly when or how the term 'Red Clydeside' came into being. The Clydesiders spoke of themselves as 'The Clydesiders' not 'Red Clydeside'. It

The legend of Red Clydeside developed during and just after the First World War as part of the political protest against what was perceived to be a war on behalf of Imperialist ruling class interests in Europe. According to Marxist historian John Foster, at the time there were those who believed that, 'the two million people of the Clyde Valley, concentrated around the biggest of Europe's heavy industry and munitions centres, represented the most serious potential threat to the existing order in Britain'.[3] One of the industrial actions that alarmed the ruling class at the time was the Forty-Hour-Week Strike of 1919: a struggle for a shorter working week as a strategy to circumvent the unemployment created by the return of the work force from the First World War. It was supported by most of the workers in the Clydeside area together with the recently demobilised soldiers, culminating in a massive demonstration in George Square on Friday 30 January 1919. Scottish veteran troops were confined by the authorities to their barracks in Maryhill for fear they would support the strikers. In the aftermath the Westminster Government, apprehensive of revolution, sent English troops and tanks into the city. Winston Churchill in particular considered it a possibility that the Bolshevik Revolution was imminent in Glasgow.[4]

Reviewing the process by which the history of the Red Clyde has been constructed, Foster describes it as, 'predictably dislocated and incoherent'.[5] He investigates the possibility that it was merely a 'heroic episode' invented by left-wing propagandists years after the event. Comparing the diverse interpretations of the period, Foster acknowledges the genuine belief of the actual participants at the time, 'that something special had occurred on the Clyde during and immediately after the First World War ... a moment of near revolutionary potential had been reached, and missed.'[6] The debate around imminent revolution in inter-war Glasgow continues into the twenty-first century, indicating the numinous quality the incident assumed in the consciousness of the city. It could be

possibly originated with Arthur Shadwell, a liberal journalist who wrote a series of articles in Journals and Newspapers about 'the Bolshevik Menace'. (Pers. Comm. Seán Damer and Irene Maver,14 May, 2010)

3   John Foster, 'Red Clyde, Red Scotland', in *The Manufacture of Scottish History* ed. Ian Donnachie and Christopher Whatley (Polygon: Edinburgh , 1992) p.107.

4   Iain McLean (1999), *The Legend of Red Clydeside*, (John Donald: Edinburgh, 1999)

5   Foster,'Red Clyde, Red Scotland'.p.118

6   Foster, Ibid. p.107.

argued that George Square 1919 became the benchmark of all future demonstrations of militancy in the city.

Foster avers that Red Clydeside passed into history during the inter-war decades as propaganda, not only for those desiring revolutionary transformation, but also for those defending the existing social system.[7] Investigating the diverse histories that went into the making of the myth of Red Clyde, he takes as his starting point the autobiographical accounts of the revolutionary leftist participants themselves: Willie Gallacher, Tom Bell, Emanuel Shinwell, Tom Johnston and David Kirkwood (although the last three later reformed and became parliamentarians). He then compares these accounts with the official ruling class records from the Ministry of Munitions: Winston Churchill, Lloyd George, and William Beveridge. This leads him on to the more recent interpreters of the phenomenon who contest the credibility of some of the claims of revolutionary threat: Keith Middlemass, James Hinton, Jeremy Cronin, Iain McLean and Alastair Reid. These theories are in turn challenged by Joseph Melling, who believes that he 'demonstrates conclusively the degree to which rank and file militancy did emerge in the later stages of the war and the degree to which previous historians had been misled by the self-serving history by the Ministry of Munitions'.[8]

Foster concludes his review of the construction of the legend of Red Clydeside by returning full circle to the original opinion in the historical debate he has outlined — that revolution was narrowly averted in 1919. But now this opinion is extrapolated, not only from the perspective of the strike leaders and government, but also from fresh evidence of the views of the owners of the means of production. The source of this most recent understanding of the circumstances leading up to Bloody Friday 1919 was the discovery in 1992 of the minute book of the Clyde Shipbuilders Association, which reported on the actual discussions that took place during the General Strike of 1919. Foster avers that it is clear from this account that the Glasgow shipyard owners, arguably the most influential force in the equation, were actually fearful of revolution. They considered the strike to be both political and dangerous because: 'It had created an active alliance between the tens of thousands of recently discharged soldiers (demobilised only weeks before in circumstances of real and threatened mutiny) and the most radical section of the industrial

7 Foster, Ibid. p.115.
8 Foster, Ibid. p.123.

workforce'.[9] The 'most radical section' refers to the shipyard workers and miners, and a strike leadership dominated by the socialist Clyde Workers Committee. In addition the bosses feared the weakness of the Glasgow civic authorities, who appeared to be sliding into collaboration and compromise with the radical elements.

However in contradistinction to Foster's conclusions based on the recorded paranoia of the shipyard owners, the memoirs of the trade union leaders themselves all reflect peaceable marchers and intentions of good faith on 30 January 1919. They also recount the reading of the Riot Act on George Square, the frenzied attack by the police on the demonstrators, the mass panic of the crowd, several of the crowd being batoned over the head including Kirkwood and Gallagher themselves, the arrests, the charges of incitement to riot, and the subsequent trials. Kirkwood's interpretation of events on the day and their aftermath is disappointingly sparse, perhaps because he himself had been rendered unconscious by a police baton. He presents no reasons for the riot or any revolutionary intent on the part of the marchers.[10] Shinwell's account is more forthcoming. Believing that the mass of workers had no aims beyond remedying the labour situation, he had addressed the Trades Council saying:

> This movement for a 40-hour week is not revolutionary in character ... it is attributable solely and entirely to the fear of possible unemployment in the near future and the desire of the workers generally to make room for the demobilized servicemen.[11]

Shinwell argues in his memoir that these views were ignored by the Press, 'which continued to report the alarmist statements of politicians who seemed able to give a graphic account of the revolutionary situation in Glasgow without coming within three hundred miles of the city'.[12] Shinwell comes to the same conclusion as did the evidence at the trial: 'the workers did not riot for the sake of making trouble: they only rioted when panic-stricken forces of law enforcement drove them to it'; and the situation became 'Red Friday' only because of the blood spilt by the police not due to imminent revolution.[13] Gallacher's memoir describes the mistrust between the

---

9   Foster, Ibid. p.124.
10 David Kirkwood, *My Life of Revolt* (George.G. Harrap: London, 1935) p.172.
11 Emanuel Shinwell, *Conflict Without Malice*, Odhams Press: London, 1955), p.61.
12 Shinwell, Ibid.P.62.
13 Shinwell,Ibid. p.65.

strike leaders, and a Press organised against the increasingly isolated strikers. His interpretation of events is the most radical, and posits the possibility of a more militant insurrection if the marchers had progressed to Maryhill to enlist the support of the Scottish troops confined to barracks there. He also admits with hindsight what he considers was the main reason for the improbability of revolution:

> We had forgotten we were revolutionary leaders of the working class. Revolt was seething everywhere, especially in the army. We had within our hands the possibility of giving actual expression and leadership to it, but it never entered our heads to do so. We were carrying on a strike when we ought to have been making a revolution.[14]

Iain McLean argues in *The Legend of Red Clydeside* (1983) that at the trial of the leaders after 'Bloody Friday' 1919, the judge and jury were not convinced that, 'any conspiracy, Bolshevist or otherwise, existed'.[15] McLean is also of the opinion that the violence in George Square was initiated by the police, who baton charged the crowd of strikers and their families together with the usual innocent bystanders who gather around any fracas in Glasgow, and was therefore what McLean labels, 'a police riot ...caused by the inexperience and incompetence of the police in handling a large crowd with no revolutionary ambitions'.[16] However the press did not believe in the innocence of the strikers' intent, with *The Glasgow Herald* reporting after the trial that the strike was, 'the first step towards the squalid terror which the world now describes as Bolshevism'.[17]

The conclusion to be drawn from the assorted first hand accounts of the event, as well as subsequent interpretations, is that the press and the police played major roles in fomenting the fear of impending revolution on Clydeside in 1919. None of the strike leaders' memoirs suggest that revolution was the plan or purpose. It is possible to argue, as does Gallagher, that the worker leaders may have been efficient industrial organisers, but they did not have the resources available to enable them to match ruling class manipulation. As a result they did not understand the true nature of the struggle in

---

14 William Gallacher, *Revolt on the Clyde* (Lawrence & Wishart: London 1936:1990). p.221.

15 McLean, *The Legend of Red Clydeside,* p.132.

16 McLean, Ibid.p.132.

17 Shinwell, *Conflict Without Malice*, p.65.

which they were involved, and were thus incapable of providing the necessary political leadership and organisation to bring about a final victory for the working class.

Politics and Protest – the 1926 General Strike

Glasgow was the centre of the 1926 General Strike in Scotland. Over the years a struggle had been developing between a growing militant working class versus the military industrial complex serving the combined interests of the land-owners, the owners of the means of production, and the State. In *Gael Over Glasgow* the history of the dispute and the build-up to the 1926 Strike creates a mood of expectation of the final showdown between Capital and Labour: 'And this fight would be decisive. For of all the long struggles and bitter industrial disputes ....this threat of a General Strike was the most serious menace Capitalism had ever been called upon to face'. (GG, pp.221-222) The novel describes the May Day march and demonstration on Glasgow Green on the eve of the strike, with a sense of euphoric certainty that the workers would triumph and the existing order overturned: 'They will see and feel the full brunt of an organised working class. ... From now on the workers will come first, as it should be. ...The old fashioned exploitation where profits come first, last and all the time is finished.' (GG, p.265) Prudence however is cautioned by the protagonist Brian the engineer who recalls the brutality of the government response to previous strikes. Evident in the text is the understanding that the police and army in the United Kingdom exist to uphold the interests of the property-owning classes, encountering little resistance from the complacent majority to the use of state sanctioned violence.

Given that Glasgow was a city with such a reputation for industrial militancy, it is surprising that the 1926 General Strike did not have the impact that might have been expected upon Glasgow, as Irene Maver argues re the events of 1926:

> The famous "Red Clydeside" ... was only marginally involved. Engineering and shipyard workers were in the "second line" of action and were not called out until the last day of the strike ... Moreover the sheer size of Glasgow made effective control difficult.[18]

---

18 Irene Maver, *Glasgow* (Edinburgh University Press: Edinburgh, 2000), pp.206-207.

The power of the media is documented for over twenty pages in *Gael Over Glasgow*. The press had joined in the strike effectively blocking the transmission of news. The press usually functions to uphold the status quo in capitalist society, but can also subvert it as in 1926. However in this instance by joining the strike its very subversion worked against its success: 'All that the Strike meant, its mammoth nature, the stranglehold it had on industry was not appreciated by the public who depended on the Press which normally linked them together.' (GG, pp.275-277) So the role of the press in 1926 was very different to the role it played to foment fear of the idea of potential Bolshevik revolution in 1919. Also in 1926 middle class volunteers stepped in to run services and break the strike, and the state was better organised than the strikers.

On 12 May 1926 the surprise call-off of the strike by the Trades Union Congress (TUC) was announced against the wishes of the miners, and without any guarantees or written terms of agreement. The reaction among the Glasgow strikers was a sense of betrayal of the workers by a leadership who had been co-opted by the ruling class,[19] articulated in *Gael Over Glasgow* as, 'after all that the Strike had been in vain with the Memorandum turned down by the miners and owners'. (GG, p.285) Contemporary writers responded quickly to the events of the time, some referring to the strike in an oblique literary form other than realism. For example Hugh MacDiarmid's now famous poem 'A Drunk Man Looks at the Thistle' published in 1926: 'I saw a rose come loupin' oot' (line 1119) refers to the labour movement rising from the image of waste, and it blooms and grows until it 'shrivelled suddenly'.[20]

Each of the five proletarian novels approaches the political unrest and the radical political movements of the era in a singular way. In contradistinction to the rather naïve enthusiasm of *Gael Over Glasgow*, and the dearth of political action in *The Shipbuilders*; *Major Operation* and *Hunger March* articulate a darker view depicting the grim reality of the unemployed workers' movement in unsentimental terms. The politics of *Major Operation* is informed by Barke's worker consciousness, articulating a Marxist internationalist attitude towards war, religion, and politics, and a more localised critique of Glasgow municipal politics and a Corporation dominated by Labour from 1933. The prevailing ethos in *No Mean City* is that of cynicism towards

19 Maver,Ibid.pp.204-205.
20 Hugh MacDiarmid, *A Drunk Man Looks at the Thistle* (1926). line 1171.

authority, and nihilism towards politics. In this novel the attitude of the authorial voice towards leftwing politics is negative. The population of Glasgow are portrayed in the novel as voting 'Red' because they were bribed, 'they sneered as they made their crosses on the ballot papers. They cared for nothing – literally nothing'. (NMC, p.70)

Gael Over Glasgow contains contradictory ideological viewpoints. On some occasions the text appears to be supporting revolution, and on others it appears fearful of it. There is a resignation in the narrative stance and a conservative acceptance of the status quo which consistently confuses and cramps the narrative attempts at a more revolutionary stance. Brian's world view is conflicted as he exhibits both admiration and disaffection towards the radical leftist politics of his fellow workers in the shipyards: 'that hot-bed of fighting socialists and agitators ...They were a daft crowd over there. It seemed they went on strike every second day'. (GG, p.106) When the ILP looms large in his life Brian dithers about whether it is the best movement to join, although he has no other political affiliation. Brian emerges as essentially apolitical preferring to head for the hills with his sandwiches than become an activist, overlooking the action rather participating in it, perhaps reflecting the title and central metaphor of the novel. This is consistent with the essentially conservative and atavistic overall vision of *Gael Over Glasgow*, harkening back to the old traditions of the Gael and a long-gone time in Scotland, a view which sits uneasily with a more radical left-wing analysis sometimes evident in the text. Recalling the history of revolutionary struggles, Brian both anticipates and fears the social revolution that seems imminent: 'And was it Britain's turn next? If they could just control it, it could be a great and worthwhile struggle...But who knows what undreamt of forces might be released in a social upheaval now?' (GG, p.148) There is an ongoing refrain throughout the novel that there are uncontrollable forces at work, a fear of organised revolution, and paranoia about communism:

> Political agitators were in their glory. ... They had their plans laid, plans of which the average working man knew little or nothing. Communists had carried out the instructions they had received years ago and had wormed their way into every working class organisation in an attempt to capture as many vital positions as possible. They awaited the revolutionary conscience awakening. (GG, p.277)

Economics and Unemployment — Hunger Marches of the 1920s & 1930s

One of the methods of civic protest documented in the novels is that of hunger marches, a phenomenon of the Great Depression and a reaction to the unemployment of 1920s and 1930s Britain. It was one of the few ways in which the unemployed, organised into the National Unemployed Workers' Movement (NUWM), could articulate their impoverishment and frustration, and attempt to regain a modicum of power through collective action.

An account of the Scottish hunger marches is contained in two volumes of collated oral histories compiled by labour historian Ian MacDougall, *Voices from the Hunger Marches: Personal Recollections of the Scottish Hunger Marchers of the 1920s and 1930s*.[21] What is most interesting about these testimonies is the matter-of-fact approach of the participants to their individual experiences. These accounts correlate with the fictionalised depictions of the marches in the realistic novels. The volumes include a timeline of the events, showing that the first Scottish hunger march occurred in 1928, even before the 1929 economic crisis which precipitated the Great Depression. The favoured destination for these marches was actually Edinburgh rather than Glasgow, although there was a significant Glasgow march in 1935, recalled by Michael Beattie, a miner from Fife: 'On the Glasgow Mairch they had cudgels ye ken, the Gorbals and the Springburn boys they had muckle cudgels. The police were afraid they wid be attacked.'[22]

Tom Clarke, an ex-professional soldier recounts: 'All Glasgow turned out. This was the great thing at that time. You could depend on at least a great demonstration.'[23] MacDougall cites *The Glasgow Herald* (25 March 1935) estimate of numbers on that march as being 40,000 demonstrators of whom 3000 were hunger marchers. These figures correspond with those given in *Hunger March* and *Major Operation*, the two novels which best document the hunger marches.

There are two major political marches described in *Major Operation*. The first march near the beginning of the novel, is a

---

21 Ian MacDougall, ed. *Voices from the Hunger Marches: Personal Recollections of the Scottish Hunger Marchers of the 1920s and 1930s*, Vol. 2 (Polygon: Edinburgh, 1990:1991), p.299.
22 MacDougall, Ibid.p.116.
23 MacDougall, Ibid.p.299.

demonstration by the NUWM against the introduction of the Means Test, instituted in 1931 to assess eligibility for unemployment insurance (see Chap 2). This was a hated, degrading procedure that caused a great deal of public protest: 'an incentive for many to support the National Unemployed Workers' Movement as a tangible expression of concern about rapidly deteriorating living standards'.[24] In *Major Operation* this march is where businessman George has a first antagonistic encounter with worker Jock who is leading his Partick contingent through the city. (MO, p.129) The irony of the situation is that as he observes the workers from the patronising perspective of his seemingly secure bourgeois position, George cannot know that Jock will soon become his friend, and that he himself (George) will soon join the ranks of the unemployed,:

> There could be no doubt about the poverty of the marchers. There didn't seem to be a really satisfactorily fed person in the ranks. They were ill-clad: quite a number in dirty rags: themselves not overclean. But they had spirit. They carried themselves proudly. Prouder still the red flags, the banners and the slogan-board. The army of the unemployed, the unemployable. (MO, p.128)

The second march occurs at the climax of *Major Operation*. (MO, pp.475-490). It is the historically realistic 'All Scotland Hunger March on the Second City'. The novel documents how from all over Scotland 250,000 workers and unemployed converged on Glasgow, forming a 'United Front Movement'. (MO, p.476) For twenty-four hours the workers put aside their divisions and take the Freedom of the City marching behind their trade union banners. There is a real sense of the power and massive scale of the hunger march, as the workers gather at George Square, and then march on to Glasgow Green bringing traffic in the city to a standstill: 'There were many miles of banners, flags and slogan-boards. It was like ten May Day processions. .... Never in its history had the Second City witnessed such a marshalling and consolidation of its organised strength.' (MO, p.482)

Major Operation contains historically realistic depictions of the NUWM of which Jock is a member, and to which he introduces his new friend George now unemployed due to the bankruptcy of his business. The history of the NUWM on Clydeside is outlined by

---

24 Maver, *Glasgow*, p. 207.

George Rawlinson,[25] who reports how its campaign for the rights of the unemployed was met with threats, intimidation and repression from the police and authorities.[26] There was lack of support and even open opposition from most trade unions, trades councils and the Labour Party in Scotland. Eventually the high profile of the movement on Clydeside and the groundswell of support for the organisation in 1930-32, 'stirred the labour establishment into action. No doubt, fearful that the NUWM were being seen as more representative of the interests of the unemployed than the trade union movement'.[27] Rawlinson argues that the fact that the NUWM remained strong and achieved so much despite the level of opposition was attributable to:

> tireless street activists like Harry McShane, and an indication that whilst unemployment was debilitating, it was possible to rally the people against such obscenities as the means test and cuts in benefits. Between the wars there were no saviours on high to deliver the unemployed from their misery. Those out of work had to rely on their own devices. This is a lesson which many are still learning.[28]

Political demonstrations in Glasgow usually had a set route aimed at the seat of civic power, the City Chambers in George Square, as delineated in *Hunger March*. However this novel articulates the bleakest most sceptical vision of the five inter-war novels as to the lack of effectiveness of such civic protest:

> So the same procedure was to be adhered to, the procedure honoured by custom and observed on every occasion by the marchers of circling the City Chambers while the councillors held their meeting. ... But it could never reach those urbane wearers of robes and chains, those arbiters of a people's destiny. It could never reach them, because they were all-powerful. (HM, p.124)

---

25 George Rawlinson, 'Mobilising the Unemployed: The National Unemployed Workers' Movement in the West of Scotland', in *Militant Workers: Labour and Class Conflict on the Clyde, 1900-1950. Essays in Honour of Harry McShane 1891-1988*, ed. Robert Duncan and Arthur McIvor. (John Donald Publishers Ltd: Edinburgh. 1992).

26 Rawlinson,Ibid.p.182.

27 Rawlinson, Ibid.p.179.

28 Quote contains an allusion to the words of 'The Internationale'. From Rawlinson, Ibid, p.193.

The massive scale and potential power of the All Scotland Hunger March is invoked in *Hunger March*, the setting for which is 24 hours on the day of the demonstration. The march converging on George Square in the centre of Glasgow is likened to an overwhelming flood: 'a vast stream of humanity was converging on the Square....a teeming deluge had engulfed the cobblestones, the pavements. It was as though the collapse of some great dam had released a torrent'. (HM, p.116) The march itself is depicted in allegorical terms as an independent entity with a life of its own: 'Driven from the rear, without pause, without fluctuation, it surged on – Black Care, Hunger, Revolt'. (HM, p.116)

However the power of the workers is held in paradox with their disempowerment; their poverty displayed in juxtaposition with the great wealth of Glasgow's industrial and entrepreneurial legacy displayed by the impressive edifices of the built environment. The starving workers have to march past the luxurious goods displayed in the windows of the city's inaccessible temples of consumption, and the narrative tone is one of disbelief at their paying no attention to the conspicuous wealth around them:

> shambling between stately frontages, between rows of lighted shops agleam with the tempting fruits of luxury trade... A place worthy of plunder, you might think, worthy of being the objective of this ragged throng; but Dull Care, Hunger and Revolt appeared as though they saw it not. (HM, p.116)

The uncharacteristic silence of the All Scotland Hunger March, so different to other marches he has witnessed, unnerves Jimmy the journalist in *Hunger March*: 'On those other occasions when he had seen them, they had created an atmosphere of spurious excitement by shouting, by waving sticks, by shrilling of fife bands.' (HM, p.122) The silence of the marchers on this occasion seems more powerful: 'You realized the grimness of it, the futility, as that pitiless line wound on and on,... the spectacle of men caught up in an inexorable machine'. (HM, p.122) The poverty and starvation of the marchers is emphasised as they 'mooch along, so mealy-mouthed, so mum. He forgot, for the moment, there were flashes in his blood that were not in theirs. He forgot that in an ill-nourished body passion does not readily catch fire.' (HM, p.123) Jimmy opines that what is needed is a war in which the unemployed could serve as cannon fodder, an ironic reference given the fact that many of them are demobilised soldiers who have received little support from the State, and the legacy of their First World War wounds is why so many of them are now: 'a pitiful multitude over which Christ Himself might have sorrowed, a multitude made up of the lame, the halt and the blind'. (HM, p.125)

The irony of the media-constructed mythology of the worker movement as 'The Terror of Red Clydeside', is exposed in the description of Buchanan Street on a busy shopping day in the 1930s:

> A procession came up the street, with blood-red banners ...These should have driven the women screaming into the basements of the shops for they bore legends in praise of Moscow, warnings about the wrath to come. 'Communists' the word flew along the pavements. But no one screamed. The men that carried the flags were broken beyond violence by the prolonged misery of unemployment and could not sustain the legends.[29]

In his novel *Magnus Merriman* (1934) Eric Linklater similarly describes a march of ex-servicemen:

> Half these ragged fellows, these slouching dole-men, these pot-bellied deformities, had once stood rigid and magnificent on parade, and marched behind the pipes with kilts swinging, ... here, with foul shirts and fouler breath, were Mars's heroes. Kings had fallen and nations perished, armies had withered and cities been ruined for this and this alone: that poor men in stinking pubs might have a great wealth of memory.[30]

This miserable state of the hunger marchers is evident in all the novels and could be posited as a contributing reason for the failure of revolution in Scotland. However in *Gael Over Glasgow* a difference is delineated between the demonstrations of the 1926 General Strike and the hunger marches of the 1930s, a difference in the development of desperation among the unemployed:

> it was not the quiet peaceful workers of the General Strike they had to deal with. But a desperate army of derelict men who had nothing to lose and a lot to gain. But oh, the shame of it, their indignation and <u>sense of bitter</u> injustice had been cruelly exploited and side-tracked

29 John R. Allan, *Scotland-1938:Twenty-Five Impressions, (Oliver &Boyd:* Edinburgh 1938) p.28.
30 Eric Linklater, *Magnus Merriman* (London, 1934:1990) p.145.

by political parties, till at last apathy and despair settled down like a huge cloud. (GG, p.311)

The idea of impending revolution is a palpable possibility in both *Major Operation* and *Hunger March*. In the former there are frequent narrative interjections articulating the hope of the proletariat anticipating, 'the day that socialism would be triumphant and lay the foundations of a new society'. (MO, p.73) This is in contradistinction to the voice of the bourgeoisie in the novel, who articulate suspicion and fear of anything that will threaten their class domination. They do not believe revolution to be a possibility in Britain anyway, it is something that happens elsewhere: 'A hunger-march was something essentially un-British: something imported from abroad – Russia.' (MO, p.237) A similar disbelief in the probability of revolution is evident in *Hunger March*: a sense that insurrection is something imported from afar: 'Had they been foreigners, you would have expected to behold, at a given signal, the flash of hidden weapons dramatically disclosed. But things like that didn't happen here.' (HM, p.121)

However the middle class observers of the march in *Hunger March*, from the safe remove of their offices, restaurants and hotels, are also fearful of Soviet-funded and inspired revolution: 'They said there was a steady stream of Soviet money coming into the country these days, that Russia was behind all the disturbances.' (HM, p.119) In both these novels, the gravitas and sense of imminent social revolution from the workers is punctuated by the chattering comments of the bourgeoisie, one moment fearful of the overturning of the existing order and the next scornful of the possibility of revolution in Britain, indicative perhaps of prevailing ambivalence and ambiguity in the contemporary zeitgeist.

The climax of *Major Operation* has George, symbolically clutching the red flag, standing over an unconscious Jock, saving his hero from the hooves of a police horse, a sacrificial leap of faith that infuses George's previously reified bourgeois existence with significance. The denouement in the final chapter consists of Jock's elegiac funeral oration for his fallen comrade in praise of his struggle and courage in allying himself with the working class. There are similarities here to the ending of Lewis Grassic Gibbon's *Grey Granite* where Chris's Communist son Ewan departs to lead the hunger march into the unanswered question of the future.[31] If the bitterly ironic lesson

31 Lewis Grassic Gibbon, *A Scots Quair* (Hutchinson & Co: London, 1946:1971).

of the First World War was 'Dulce et decorum est pro patria mori' (It is right and fitting to die for your country), then not only had it been learnt, but it re-surfaced again and again in the contemporary outlook and literature of the inter-war period.

Revolutionary Deterrents

The ruling class in any society maintains its domination through ideological hegemony and the consent of the majority, and only resorts to the coercive apparatus of law and order as a last resort (discussion in Chapter 5). When ideology failed, the British State was in a unique position to control insurrection by force with the most powerful Imperial army since the Romans, having had centuries of practice in policing the colonies and quelling revolts in Ireland, Africa, America, Asia, Ireland, and of course Scotland itself. In Glasgow this acted as a coercive deterrent to worker revolution, along with arrest of the worker leadership. The main symbolic figure of Red Clydeside was John Maclean, the Glasgow teacher and Marxist leader of the British Socialist Party; twice imprisoned for his opposition to the First World War. [32] In *Major Operation*, Maclean is described as, 'the indomitable, incorruptible first Scottish representative of the Soviet Union.' (MO, p.481) In 1918 Maclean was arrested and found guilty of sedition in one of the greatest political trials in Scottish history. And in 1925 the entire Polit Bureau of the Communist Party of Great Britain was arrested and received prison sentences just prior to the impending General Strike. However the failure of the Trades Union Congress to satisfactorily resolve the 1926 General Strike was popularly perceived to be a betrayal of the workers by a leadership who had lost their nerve and been co-opted by the ruling class.[33] Brian voices the prevailing disillusionment and cynicism in *Gael Over Glasgow*: 'all the past had been squalor, misery and exploitation, and brave gallants only dupes of imperialistic aggression; and the working people little less than blind dull slaves.' (GG, p.132)

Throughout *Major Operation*, Jock, the worker leader, attempts to politically educate bourgeois George, who is initially screened from the truth of state sanctioned violence by the ingrained ideology of his inherent class position: 'He was completely ignorant of the brutal

32 John Broom, *John Maclean*, (MacDonald Publishers: Loanhead, 1973)
33 John Foster, 'Scotland and the Russian Revolution' in *Scottish Labour History Society*, 23, (1988).

and ruthless dictatorship of monopoly capital'.(MO, p.366)   The realities of British Imperialism, what is referred to sardonically in the second sentence of the novel as, 'The Empire on which the sun never sets', (MO, p.341) is also the Empire upon which the blood has never set. George has no understanding of how the lifeblood of subaltern classes is bartered in the name of power, as Jock attempts to explain it to him during one of their consciousness-raising sessions:

> When the capitalist state finds out that it can't govern unless our blood's shed – then they'll have no hesitation in shedding it. There won't be any nonsense about democracy the moment the will of the British People cuts across the interests of the governing class. (MO, p. 341)

As a small-time capitalist conformist, George cannot understand the dark power brought to bear upon any opposition to the imperial British state. It is only in the closing scenes of the novel, when he saves Jock's life that the actuality of the situation becomes apparent to George, and he has his moment of epiphany and glory, holding the red flag as he sacrifices himself under the hooves of a police horse to save his comrade.

The rhetoric of blood was much associated with the inter-war period because of the legacy of the First World War, during which the British military-industrial complex did not hesitate to sacrifice the working class on the battlefield, or to ruthlessly repress those workers who offered any challenge to their authority. All the novels, written with the First World War and its consequences still fresh in living memory, contain a subtext of the sense of the devastating impact of the so-called 'Great War', the death-dealing from which no class had been immune. Johnnie in *No Mean City* talks of how the working classes breed 'fodder for the capitalist cannons'. (NMC, p.112) Even Arthur Joyce, the arch-capitalist in *Hunger March*, had been seemingly protected from the 'harsh blows' of fate, until the death of his own son in the war. (HM, p.28)

The Westminster Government had a long history of violently suppressing the rebellious Scots to draw upon when it came to dealing with Red Clydeside. The aftermath of Bloody Friday at George Square 1919 is described in *Gael Over Glasgow* and contains an understanding of the relationships between political coercion and economic ownership, and the complacency of the masses:

They had machine gun nests rigged up along the docks. What for?
The Germans? They had troops parading in full war kit through the
city. Our city! Could anything be more outrageous than that. There
should have been a wave of indignation throughout the country at
that and whoever had ordered those troops out should have been
kicked into the Clyde for the coward he was. But no; the people stood
for it. Of course it was to protect property. (GG, p.266)

During the General Strike of 1926, the solidarity of the Glasgow
workers and the widespread class-consciousness was so threatening
to the British Government, that it sent seven naval vessels to the Clyde
in an attempt to intimidate the strikers. There was extensive anger at
the conduct of the police who had been given extra powers, including
the ability to prevent public meetings. As occurred in 1919, there
were instances of police brutality and forcible breaking up of strike
meetings, and hundreds were arrested during the nine days of the
strike. So the legal system came to be regarded by the workers as an
instrument of class oppression.[34] In *Major Operation* Jock argues for
the great power that could be exercised by the workers, if only they
could become conscious of how the forces of armed imperialism
(army and police) maintaining the dominance of those in power are
(ironically) recruited from within their own subordinate class.

We are the armed forces ... we are the Nation. If we take our power
openly and firmly, realising clearly what we are doing and what we
want, who the hell's going to gainsay us? ... if we sit back and trust
to the honour and decency of our class enemies, then we will be
drowned in a sea of our own blood.(MO, p.343)

Although there were very real fears from both the Westminster
Government and Glasgow Industrialists in 1919 that, left unchecked,
the workers' uprising would turn into a revolution, accounts from the
time and subsequent analysis cast doubt upon this possibility. There
are conflicting opinions offered in examples of other novels from the
inter-war period (which do not fit into the realistic proletarian model
analysed here). William Bolitho's journalistic novel of slum tourism
entitled *Cancer of Empire* (1924), while sensationally purporting
to include information from 'the Clyde Reds themselves', cites
abysmal social conditions in Glasgow as being sufficient grounds for

revolution.[34] In contradistinction John Buchan's novel *Mr Standfast* (1919) reflects a contrary opinion towards the possibility of the revolutionary potential of the Glasgow proletariat: 'They may crack about their Industrial workers and the braw things they're going to do, but there's a wholesome dampness about the tinder on Clydeside. They should try Ireland.'[35]

In *An Industrial Survey of the South West Scotland*, a report produced for the Board of Trade in 1932, it was noted with concern that altogether no new internal investments had come to the Clyde during the previous decade. The authors of the report directly relate this to an impression that 'the district is one seething with unrest which is of a subversive character'. [36] However the report also debunks this perception, arguing that, 'while there is a small amount of Communism', this had little influence over the 'mass of working people', of which 'no more steady and dependable body is to be found in any similar area'.[37] Although the Clyde shipyards have long been regarded as the cradle of the radical labour movement in Scotland, it is a moot point whether shipbuilding was the main nurturing ground of radicalism, given the defensive nature of shipyard trade unionism with its job demarcation and protectionist strategies. Indeed there was a range of influences, and mining has far more of a claim to the title of revolutionary cradle, with James Keir Hardie famously a product of the Lanarkshire and Ayrshire coalfields.[38]

Hunger March posits the idea of how the social deprivation of the slums is a breeding ground for revolutionaries: 'those elements composed a fine marching tune for revolutionaries. With that in his ears, a man might fling a bomb into the innermost ring of the capitalists and harken unafraid to the roar of its bursting.' (HM, pp.209-210) In contrast to this belief, historian Sydney Checkland suggests that the Glasgow slums were places so destructive of humanity that they were unlikely to produce organised and sustained protest.[39] Alastair

---

34 William Bolitho, *The Cancer Of Empire* (London: G. Putnam, 1924) concerns events in Glasgow prior to the First World War, so outwith the defined time frame for this analysis.

35 John Buchan, *Mr Standfast,* (Oxford University Press, 1919, repr.1993),p.60.

36 Board of Trade. *An Industrial Survey of the South West of Scotland,* (Political Economy Department of the University of Glasgow. HMSO: London. 1932).p.140

37 Board of Trade. Ibid, p.140.

38 Irene Maver. Pers. comm. University of Glasgow. May 2009.

39 Sydney Checkland, *The Upas Tree: Glasgow 1875-1975* (University of Glasgow Press: Glasgow 1977) p.32.

Reid argues 'there were small groups of genuine revolutionaries in the area' and 'some more influenced by industrial syndicalism', but that, 'the main political catalyst and then beneficiary of these agitations was the generally more moderate and constitutionalist ILP'. He concludes with the relevant point that,

> Perhaps one of the longest legacies of red (sic) Clydeside was the way in which John Maclean and Jimmy Maxton were more widely and fondly remembered than their more moderate and representative colleagues: as part of a long tradition of romanticizing Scottish history, the rebels and the martyrs were generally preferred to the practical politicians.[40]

Possible reasons for the failure of worker revolution are contained within the texts of the realist novels. Brian in *Gael Over Glasgow* predicts that the reason why there will be no revolution is because the workers prefer, 'Charlie Chaplin and a pint of beer...and the other little things that made life worth while to the man at the bench'(GG, p.285) (the notion of false consciousness as deterrent to revolution is discussed in Chapter Five). *Major Operation* contains a contemptuous diatribe on the betrayal of the working class by the leadership of the labour movement who are viewed as selling out, co-opted and corrupted: 'There was the record of heroic struggle on the part of the workers and the grossest, most shameless betrayal by their so-called leaders'. (MO, p.386) When George's romantic notions of revolutionary working class heroes are debunked by mundane reality it causes him disillusionment and despair in *Major Operation*:

> From considering them abstractly, as a theoretical proletariat – the advance guard of history – to seeing them as men and women standing around corners, living in squalid tenements, drinking in mean and horrible public houses, going to football matches and dog racing. (MO, pp.387-388)

---

40 Alastair J. Reid, 'Red Clydesiders' (1915-1924), *Oxford Dictionary of National Biography*. (Oxford University Press, 2004-6). pp.2-3.

Conclusion

Political action, and the underlying forces behind it, differed between the major moments of political turbulence in Glasgow in 1919, 1926, and the 1930s. However, by most accounts, a common denominator between the instances of unrest was an ambivalence of aspiration, from the main actors involved, towards actually deposing the prevailing social order. The threat of coercion from a powerful British Imperial army and police force would have been a restraint on revolutionary momentum, thus it is possible that the movement towards social transformation became another casualty of British Imperialism: a complex project in which many Scots across the classes were willing participants. Despite the extensive socialist worker education programmes organized on Clydeside during the inter-war era, it is also possible that the greatest deterrent to revolutionary aspiration may have been false consciousness, as argued in the following chapter.

5   Consciousness and the City

Ideological Hegemony and False Consciousness

Introduction

The five realist novels present a convincing voice reflecting many of the daily concerns and material realities of life in inter-war Glasgow. They also permit an insight into the ideological hegemony of the era, and how it influenced individual consciousness in a manner that arguably persists into the twenty-first century. The leftwing leanings of many of the characters in the novels originate in the alienation and disempowerment of their class position; evidence for why Clydeside remained, for more than seventy years after the events depicted in the novels, the heartland of the Scottish Labour Party. The novels, to a greater or lesser degree, chart their protagonists' journey towards a point of social and political realisation, although sometimes this is a recognition of impotence. Despite their circumstances many of the characters are aspirational, not just in terms of political will, but in their desire to better their standing within the class structure: to move from the working class to the middle class. As well as political awareness, the novels all acknowledge the socio-economic foundation which informs the political motivations and choices of the characters. This chapter considers whether false consciousness was a reason for the failure of the ongoing class struggle to evolve nascent revolutionary potential in Glasgow during the inter-war era, and how this supposition may be substantiated by the novels.

False Consciousness

The possibility of overturning the existing order by revolutionary means in the 1930s (as in 1919 and 1926) was curtailed by the threat of force from a powerful British Imperial army. But there were also the economic and social restrictions reinforcing the status quo, as well as the ideological conditioning — the powerful hegemony of the capitalist state and the attendant false consciousness.[1] An aspect of

---

1   A concept used in Marxist analysis although not a term ever used by Marx himself.

this in a capitalist culture is the inculcated desire to 'better oneself', to 'escape' the material conditions of poverty, to join the system rather than fight it. If social status is perceived as bestowing the ability to control one's destiny, then it becomes desirable to increase one's status in the social hierarchy.

The concept of ideological hegemony theorizes the way in which relationships of domination and exploitation are embedded, internalized and consensual in society, inducing 'false consciousness'. Georges Lukács was one of the first to develop these constructs derived from a Marxist theory of social class, locating them within the framework of reification and alienation of social relations in a capitalist system.[2] The concept of false consciousness refers to the manner in which material and institutional processes in capitalist society are misleading to both bourgeoisie and proletariat, albeit in different ways. The mental representations of the ruling class are unable to understand the true nature of the capitalist system or the reasons for its crises; and those of the oppressed class are unable to understand how the reified social relations around them systematically both embody and obscure the realities of their own subordination, exploitation, and domination. For example when members of an underclass unwittingly adopt the views and values of an oppressor class, or fail to comprehend the arbitrariness, irrationality and inhumanity of the reified system of social relations.[3]

Terry Eagleton insists on the importance of grasping the precise meaning for Marxism of ideology, the function of which is to legitimate and perpetuate the power of the ruling class, or the owners of the means of production, in any society.[4] Eagleton credits Lukács's *History and Class Consciousness* (1923) for reintroducing social consciousness to a Marxism previously dominated by the notion of economic determinism (the idea that social relations are not a matter of freedom of choice but a constraint of material necessity). Eagleton avers that for Lukács, social consciousness, in particular the class consciousness of the proletariat, is not just a reflection of social conditions, but a transformative force within them: 'Capitalist society in general is ridden with reification ... but it is in the interests

---

2   Georges Lukács, *History and Class Consciousness; Studies in Marxist Dialectics.* (MIT Press: Cambridge,Mass. 1920, 1971), p.83-222.
3   Lukács Ibid.
4   Terry Eagleton, *Marxism and Literary Criticism,* (Methuen: London, 1976) p.6

of a subject class ... to grasp that social order in its dynamic totality, and in doing so it becomes conscious of its own commodified status'.[5]

During the first decades of the twentieth century the labour movement in Scotland offered an educational counterbalance to the ideological hegemony of the capitalist system. The Socialist Sunday School movement and the Clarion Scouts were organisations formed to educate young people in socialist principles.[6] Class awareness amongst the workers was raised through left wing political newspapers such as *Forward, Justice, Clarion, Vanguard* and *The Socialist*; and through the Outdoors Movement. Socialist study groups and night schools offered classes in Marxist economics and history, tutors and students of which would go on to play important roles in Red Clydeside (one of these tutors was John Maclean). From a critical right wing perspective *Mr Standfast* (1919) by John Buchan contains a depiction of Red Clydeside and socialist education as a foreign import inappropriate to Glasgow: 'Thae young lads are all drucken-daft with their wee books about Cawpital and Collectivism... Them and their socialism!...all that foreign trash...the world is getting socialism now like the measles.'[7]

A left leaning influence and somewhat Marxist interpretation is apparent in much of the writing from the inter-war era, manifest in the Condition of Scotland discourse, and strongly evident in *Major Operation* and a little less so in *Gael Over Glasgow* and *Hunger March*. There are references to the counter hegemonic education for workers and the unemployed mentioned throughout *Major Operation* and *Gael Over Glasgow*. In *Hunger March* working class Joe Humphry becomes conscientised to the oppression of his class when he reads Marx: 'His outlook might be said to have been circumscribed by the slant of the tenements opposite. It was not until he was adolescent that ...Marxian writers ...Communist agitators, gathering together in his mind, illumined it with a sudden burst of light.'(HM, p.69)

Edwin Muir argues that socialism did the most in the late nineteenth and early twentieth centuries to humanise the social conditions of the working class in Scotland although, 'The very poor are almost more hard to convert to Socialism than the very rich ...

5   Terry Eagleton, (ed.) *Ideology* (Longman: London, 1994) p.12
6   W. Hamish Fraser. 'The Working Class', in Fraser and Irene Maver (eds), *Glasgow, Volume II:1830-1912* (Manchester University Press, 1996), pp.338-339.
7   John Buchan, *Mr Standfast* (Oxford University Press: Oxford,.1919:1993), p.54.

partly because they are too sunk in hopelessness to open their minds to an idea, and partly because they cherish their exclusiveness as something which has become necessary to them.'[8] There is little class solidarity in *No Mean City*, with characters like Peter Stark who 'was not truly interested in any possible reorganisation of society itself, but only in his own escape from the unsuccessful poverty-stricken masses of poor fools who constituted the proletariat.' (NMC, p.106)

Marxist literature had not previously been on failed business man George Anderson's reading list in *Major Operation*, so he does not understand the dialectical forces at work and is ignorant of the true nature of social relationships, 'All his life he had lived in a fool's paradise, sheltered and screened from reality, taking refuge behind the shams and the illusions of his class'. (MO, p.357) In Jock's opinion, this makes George an 'utterly bewildered bourgeois'. (MO, p.319) Jock's greatest difficulty in his re-education of George is to 'convince him of the class nature of society'. (MO, p.292) Nevertheless, it is through re-education that false consciousness can sometimes be overcome, as George discovers when Jock introduces him to a Marxist reading programme: 'As he began to grasp clearly the class nature of society' he realises that 'There were terrific class battles raging at the moment.' (MO, p.385)

Scouring the scales of bourgeois idealism from George's eyes is tough work for Jock, who lectures his new pupil in class solidarity: 'Once you're unemployed ... you'll find yourself an outcast and a pariah unless you get into the ranks of the organized unemployed and fight there, shoulder to shoulder, with your unemployed comrades.' (MO, p.338) Even so, when George eventually arrives at a comprehension of the true character of class relationships he also becomes conscious of the betrayal of the labour movement by the Labour Party and the schisms within the Left, replete with its own form of false consciousness and inner contradictions.

The false consciousness of loyalty to capitalist employers, whose main concern is their profit margins, is debunked in *Hunger March*. Boss Arthur Joyce has not told his employees of the imminent closure of his business, but some of them guess it. Celia Ker, his secretary is incredulous when first hearing the rumours that 'Joyce's would be the next big firm, if things didn't look up, to find themselves in Queer Street'. (HM, p.112) Now she views her employer with a new

8   Edwin Muir, *Scottish Journey* (Mainstream Publishing Company: Edinburgh. 1935:1979), p.97

understanding of his pending perfidy towards his employees: 'had he considered what it would mean to all those people who had trusted him, all those who had worked under him, who had flung their hearts, their souls, their interests into Joyce's.' (HM, p.113) However the novel does end on a more positive note when Arthur Joyce has a change of heart and decides to keep the firm in business.

There is also a lack of awareness of the exploitative nature of class relationships in *The Shipbuilders*. Danny's devotion to his boss Leslie is expressed in his repeated refrain with regard to Leslie throughout the novel as 'A toff and a gentleman'. Danny's 'admiration of Leslie Pagan was flawless... his decent working man's sense of respect for a good and efficient master' who he adores and trusts 'with a faith almost religious'. (SH, p.17)

However it is hard to avoid a sense that there is some form of false consciousness at work in Danny's attitude. At a liminal moment in British society when the structure of class devotion was becoming obsolete, Danny's faith in his master remains anachronistically undiminished: 'Whatever happened, the boss would see him right and give him work to do and decent pay for that work'. (SH, p.17) But his master ultimately betrays Danny's misplaced trust in order to pursue his own class interests. There is no sense of a political consciousness of the workers in *The Shipbuilders*, and little sense of the tremendous political battles and class struggles that were taking place in Clydeside during the inter-war era. There is only a brief mention when Danny is walking the streets: 'In a side street near Byres Road a noisy speaker on behalf of the National Unemployed Workers' Movement was hoarsely proclaiming communism to a quiet, if occasionally facetious, knot of people'.(SH, p.26) In its unquestioning acceptance of unequal class and power relationships, and its sense of the powerlessness of the individual to act as a subjective agent against the economic forces of capitalism, *The Shipbuilders* could be judged as an embodiment of false consciousness in itself and a reinforcement of the status quo, conveying a sense of the irrelevance of individual struggles against larger class interests.

In the West of Scotland a particular form of false consciousness exists in the sectarian divisions inherent in the society between Catholic and Protestant. These were more pronounced in the inter-war years than they are at the start of the twenty-first century. In times of economic hardship there is an increasing awareness of such divisions within a society and it is surprising that the novels do not make more reference to this. Possibly the best description of this sectarian schism is contained in *The Shipbuilders*, at a match between Rangers and Celtic Glasgow's two leading football teams known locally as 'The Old Firm', representing:

> the dark significance of sectarian and rival passions. Blue for the Protestants of Scotland and Ulster, green for the Roman Catholics of the Free State ... All the social problems of a hybrid city were to be sublimated in the imminent clash of mercenaries'. (SH, pp.66-67)

Notwithstanding the prevailing romanticism and mythology that surrounds the beautiful game, *The Shipbuilders* articulates an understanding that the warrior tradition in Scotland obfuscates the fact that football, like war, is a capitalist commercial enterprise based on the profit incentive.

Capitalism could not continue without the consent of the workers. Working class solidarity would be a threat to the British ruling class who perfected the old Roman strategy of divide and rule, both in its colonial empire and in its home industries. In *No Mean City* the Gorbals' characters judge their neighbours in terms of how they dress and speak and the street in which they live. These divisions within the working class are a form of false consciousness and undermine any hope of working class solidarity in the novel. The multifaceted, encoded nuances of Gorbals' social hierarchies are delineated in the novel:

> society in the tenements is graded far more narrowly than in the outside world. One street may be definitely "better class" than another and not such good class as a third. Families that have two rooms look down upon those that live in a "single end". (NMC, p.104)

Divisions within the working class are also mapped out in *Gael Over Glasgow*. When Brian finds work as a fitter in the Singer sewing machine factory in Clydebank, it is dominated by a work ethic in which the machine operators are set against the fitters or engineers. He understands 'It was only natural grousing against their unnatural existence.'(GG, p.245) Racism is another form of false consciousness. Brian's workmate labels the machinists as 'white coolies' in a reference to British Colonialism. (GG, p.246) He exhorts Brian to '"Remember the old colour bar. No proud fitter should associate with these low coolies. Remember the white man's burden. Don't forget you're a pukka sahib"'. (GG, p.257) As in the other inter-war texts, class solidarity does not imply inter-race solidarity.

In the labour hierarchy of inter-war Glasgow, first generation Irish and Highlanders were relegated the lower status jobs and 'anti-Gael phobia' is referred to throughout *Major Operation*. A form of false consciousness occurs when the marginalised internalise their oppression and turn against their own class, evident in how the shipyard foreman, only two generations removed from his own Highland roots: 'would rather have a gang of Chinese or coolies than Highlandmen'. (MO, p.39) Also, as previously alluded to, there is much religious prejudice against 'the papes' – the name given to those from Irish or Highland roots.[9] This reflects a reality in the West of Scotland where the Protestant population historically held an elite position in the job hierarchy and had privileged access to employment and promotion over Catholics. The depiction of a worker movement divided along sectarian lines in Glasgow is very different from Marx's vision of international working class solidarity as embodied in the philosophy of internationalism and 'workers of the world unite'. Barke is offering the reader a reminder of 'How the workers were beaten in one country and successful in another was of the greatest importance.' (MO, p.385)

If the dominant prejudice against Highlanders in inter-war Glasgow was one of 'Gaelic decadence', then *Gael Over Glasgow* represents an attempt to reclaim the importance of the Highland roots of Clydeside, an aspect of the inter-war revival of nationalist sentiment. However it is this feature of the novel that places it at risk of descending into what Barke labels in *Major Operation* as 'The Tartan Ragstore of Romance'.(MO, p.81) The narrative voice of Barke's own realism contains contradictory messages towards the Gaelic past. On the one hand nostalgia and regret at the passing of a culture, and on the other contempt for contemporary attempts at cultural revival:

> The Gael could not survive into a world of expanding capitalist production...To what purpose had the Gael lived and fought and died?...To hand down to posterity a corpus of classical instrumental music to be prostituted at Highland Gatherings? (MO, p.96)

---

9   'The papes' meaning papists or Catholics, incorrectly applied to Highlanders who were not all Catholic.

Alcohol, along with its attendant social problems, as an escape from daily life is an underlying theme throughout the five inter-war novels. Together with gambling and other forms of escapism from reality, alcohol is in itself a form of false consciousness, a substitutive satisfaction for a more meaningful existence. Alcohol is omnipresent in the novels and consumed in a quasi-medicinal manner as an antidote to the more unpleasant realities of life in Glasgow. In *Major Operation* the anonymous voice of a Glasgow 'jakey' [10] articulates the problem: 'Been a Jake drinker in my day. Meth, lavender water, green paint. Pain in the guts now. Think of the money spent on drink that might bring back a fortune'. (MO, pp.121-122) And later in the novel, 'Get drunk for one night and drown the misery... Six sleepless nights of misery and one night blotto! Takes effect quicker on an empty stomach'. (MO, p.380) Likewise the 'Escape Complex' in *No Mean City* echoes like a refrain throughout the novel. It refers to the desire of the slum dwellers to block out the grim reality of their existence and is achieved mostly through alcohol.[11] A descriptive passage in the novel conveys a sense of sociological prescription on the part of the authorial voice:

> Battles and sex are the only free diversions in slum life. Couple them with drink, which costs money, and you have the three principal outlets for that escape complex which is for ever working in the tenement dweller's subconscious mind. Johnnie Stark would not have realised that the 'hoose' he lived in drove him to the streets or that poverty and sheer monotony drove him in their turn into the pubs and the dance halls or into affairs. (NMC, p.44)

In *Major Operation* the device of the hospital permits Barke, not only to present the reader with a cross-section of Glasgow society, but also to demonstrate the effects of endemic alcohol abuse amongst the Glaswegian working class. Many of the characters in the ward with George and Jock are suffering the ill health caused by a lifetime of sustained alcohol consumption: stomach ulcers and liver damage. Despite the knowledge that the drink will result in their demise, they obsess over their release date from hospital and the return to the

---

10 Homeless alcoholic person.
11 This avoidance 'Escape Complex' is different from the aspirational desire of characters in the novel to escape their class position, discussed earlier in this chapter.

pub. An illustration of this is a passage in which one of the inmates on George's ward explains his fellow patients:

> You've got to understand how these fellows were brought up and how they live. If there were no pubs there would be a revolution in a month. That's why the government won't allow prohibition…Booze is the safety valve of the British nation. (MO, p.225)

The novel *Major Operation* contains an understanding of the dominant role of alcohol in proletarian Glaswegian life and its role as a deterrent to revolution. The narrative lapses periodically into what appears to be an Irish accent to articulate this: 'There'll never be any Red Clyde so long as there's Red Biddy.[12] Ah, the bhoys would rather have a night with Red Biddy than a night with Burns.' (MO, p.121) Alcohol is a great opiate of the masses and the social problems related to alcohol are as prevalent in Glasgow of the twenty-first century as they were during the inter-war period.

Class Consciousness and Conflict

The First World War acted as a conscientising exercise regarding the true nature of class-exploitation; experience of the trenches had sowed the seeds of doubt regarding the existing order and obedience to the ruling elite, and those who returned home disseminated that awareness. The shipbuilding industry however was traditionally paternalistic, hierarchical and authoritarian, controlled by a coterie of Edwardian patriarchs into, and even beyond, the inter-war era. Leslie's relationship with his own father reflects this in *The Shipbuilders*, and although not an authoritarian, he himself is tormented by his overdeveloped sense of responsibility towards his workers, echoing an officer's war-time concern for his men, 'those rough innocents whose destinies were so strangely in his hands'. (SH, p.8) *The Shipbuilders* reflects no radical class-consciousness on the part of the authorial voice. The two protagonists are representations of their classes -employer and employee, and the resulting uneven relationship could be viewed as patronising on the part of Leslie the boss, and sycophantic on the part of Danny the worker. The fact that these characters knew each other in the army is significant – both

---

12 Red Biddy was a popular cheap alcoholic drink in Glasgow concocted from mixing red wine and methanol.

seek to retain the status quo in their relationship but find it impossible because of the changing economic landscape. As with many of the de-mobbed population, they simply do not fit into the shifting world order in which they find themselves. Theirs is an unusual and anachronistic relationship. Leslie's sense of responsibility towards Danny and 'the best part of a thousand men' makes him desperate to save the shipyard so that these men will not be, 'put out on the dole, to hang about street corners, to be denied their right to work, to know emptiness indescribable!' (SH, p.10) Liberal guilt seems strangely out of place during the trauma of the Great Depression, and is possibly more appropriate to the philosophy of social harmony that had characterised pre-war Liberalism in Glasgow, which had fractured by the inter-war period.

The methods by which the protagonists in *The Shipbuilders* are able to deal with the effects of the Depression are determined by their class position. At the close of the narrative, bourgeois Leslie can use his surplus capital to abdicate his responsibility for his workers, sell the shipyard, escape the depressed north and relocate south to England. Danny is trapped in Glasgow by his poverty, but reinvents himself as a vendor of wood: ironically becoming a small business man in his own right. Both of these strategies reflect the actual economic trends of the time, with the movement of capital to the south-east of the United Kingdom, and the necessity for working men to reinvent themselves in new and different employment in Glasgow.

In *Major Operation* when the protagonists meet in hospital they have been reduced to an equal social status by their ill-health, unemployment, and poverty. In the opening chapters George Anderson is described as a bankrupt coal agent. (MO, p.141) His opposite number in the narrative, both in the hospital ward and in terms of class position, is Jock MacKelvie, 'leading hand of the squad of red leaders' (who painted the ships with red lead). (MO, p.31) Ironically Jock is also a 'Red Leader' of the workers' movement, well liked and respected by his workplace and political comrades. The humorous observation of the surgeon in the hospital is that Jock goes, 'from red leader to Red Leader'. (MO, p.183) Being unskilled and casual workers, the red leaders were at the bottom of the class-hierarchy of the shipyards having no job security and 'not every day did he enjoy three full and satisfying meals'.(MO, p.77) Jock and George meet in Glasgow's 'Eastern Hospital a public, charitable institution', (MO, p.145) possibly modelled on the Glasgow Royal Infirmary. In the 1930s a member of George's class would normally have used private healthcare, [13] but after his bankruptcy he 'had to confess he couldn't afford a nursing home'. (MO, p.145) Jock becomes a persuasive influence on George's class consciousness and, by the final chapters of the novel, in a passionate declaration of faith he has converted to being a member of the working class movement and 'a Red' himself.

The narrative of *Major Operation* is permeated with class-consciousness on the part of both proletariat and bourgeoisie. The middle class are contemptuous of anyone they consider to be of lower social status, and the working class scorn the effete nature of the middle class. The attitude of the working class towards the bourgeoisie is that they are: 'fearful of risk'. (MO, p.116) This is an ironic reversal of the usual view of entrepreneurs as being risk takers. After the failure of George's business his economic hardship situates him, 'between the world of the Haves and the world of the Have-nots'. (MO, p.329) As Jock, his new worker comrade, observes, George was 'pressed down into the ranks of the working class'.(MO, p.339) When George finally understands the reality of his position he is, 'as fit to face life as a pampered poodle'. (MO, p.356) There is an ongoing Marxist critique in the novel of the parasitic nature of the middle classes, and the sustenance of their lifestyle through exploiting the surplus value of the workers. Particular condemnation is reserved for middle class women such as George's wife Mabel: 'As a lady, her position was maintained by the wage-slavery of some forty human beings. Thus she was never devoid of clothes, food, shelter or entertainment'. (MO, p.216) Mabel in turn looks down on anyone she considers of inferior social status, and before the failure of his business even George her husband, 'who prided himself on his general democratic broad-mindedness', complies passively with her social snobbery, 'the innate superiority of class over class'. (MO, p.53)

Class divisions are constantly emphasised and commented on in *Hunger March* with an ironic judgement of the middle class and sympathy towards the workers. The bourgeois observers of the hunger march, sitting passively inside the aptly named luxury restaurant overlooking George Square are referred to as: 'The window-gazers inside the Palatial'. (HM, p.119) The narrative voice

13 The British National Health Service with free health care for all was created in 1948.

is supportive of the working class marchers, and so accordingly is ironic in its expression of the middle class opinions of the voyeuristic diners critiquing the marchers.

Class conflict is understood in a different way by the somewhat naïve narrative perspective of Brian in *Gael Over Glasgow*. With reference to the government's refusal to accept the Sankey Report on the miners' plight (discussed in Chapter Four), 'It was a disgrace and could only create class hatred. A handful of mine owners preferred and protected against the Nation ... this stupid class hatred was only going to make things worse in the long run'. (GG, p.107) Brian wonders why the classes cannot cooperate between themselves to solve the economic problems of the nation as they had done during the First World War, and 'class war' is referred to. (GG, p.268) The fear of class-slippage, of falling further down the ladder of working class life is omnipresent in *No Mean City*, and both Johnnie and his brother Peter marry girls who are of higher social status than themselves, described as being 'better class'. (NMC, p.105)

The class system in Glasgow is as rigid as anywhere else in the United Kingdom. However Scotland has always had greater problems of poverty and social deprivation than its southern neighbour. Access to housing, education, nutrition, health, and life-expectancy were, and still are, determined by class in Scotland. However, despite social deprivation and enormous class differentials in inter-war Glasgow, Sydney Checkland argues that 'there appears to have been a minimum of class-consciousness, much less overt class conflict'. He offers a reason for this as being in the 'spatial segregation of the classes' due to the physical structure of the city that separated classes into different residential areas.[14] (Discussed in Chapter Three.)

Individual Agency versus Economic Determinism

Mostly the characters in the novels are depicted as having little individual agency and are portrayed as being determined and coerced by socio-economic forces that are beyond their control. This individual passivity in itself would have been a deterrent to cohesive working class revolutionary action. Is there any way forward for the individual within such circumstances? The novels illustrate that then, as now, there are great differences between the classes regarding the

---

14 Sydney Checkland, *The Upas Tree: Glasgow 1875-1975,* (University of Glasgow Press: Glasgow 1977) p.32.

control they have over their lives, and this is usually dependent on degrees of economic security.

The Shipbuilders could be judged as an attempt to reinforce the status quo in its unquestioning acceptance of unequal class power relationships, and its sense of the powerlessness of the individual to act against the economic forces of capitalism. There is a feeling of the irrelevance of individual struggles against larger class interests. Although Leslie would like to help Danny, he seems unable to help even himself, and Danny simply accepts, 'With the simple realism of his kind he knew that he was helpless under the great machine'. (SH, p.17) There is a sense of economic determinism, of the inability of bosses and workers alike to prevent the economic crisis: 'Danny could yet not escape that obsessing sense of calamity impending. Something big and black had happened, never mind why...there brooded over him the realisation that the old, safe life was falling to pieces about him'. (SH, p.85) The fatalism and futility of individual agency in the face of powerful extrinsic forces is experienced more intensely by Leslie in *The Shipbuilders* when his aged father becomes ill: 'There was upon him a queer, dumb feeling that fate was setting the scene for his trial and decision with an almost artistic care.' (SH, p.115) His father has been unable to face the truth of the near bankruptcy of his business and will talk, 'of anything save the likelihood of the Pagan partnership being broken up'. (SH, p.116)

The parallel plot structure in *The Shipbuilders* illustrates the effects of economic uncertainty on the emotions of the male characters, comparing the passive guilt and defeatism of employer Leslie the shipyard owner; with the helpless disintegration of employee Danny the riveter into unemployment, drunkenness, violence and imprisonment. Both characters are anachronisms, portrayed as morally strong but economically weak, caught up by forces they do not understand and over which they have no power. Both are trapped by economic necessity in an unjust system. Both are living with delusions and denial about their lives. The consciousness of the characters cannot comprehend the complexity of their changing conditions, and the narrative voice is seemingly complicit in the confusion, never managing to analyse the implications of their position in the broader economic context.

The Edwardian capitalist Arthur Joyce in *Hunger March* considers himself to be above economic vagaries as a member of the ruling class.

Business has been a fixed point for his life compass, as he reflects on a life described in a mixture of existential metaphors: 'Had he ever been a slave to business? ... Like the moon at nightfall, it had been a definite object in a vague windy space. You steered the ship of your existence according to it.' (HM, p.101) The authorial voice in *Hunger March* criticises modernity and the passive consumer consciousness of capitalism and Arthur's secretary, Celia, is 'an unwitting victim of mass-production'. (HM, p.54) Mrs Humphry, Arthur's cleaner in *Hunger March*, is conscious of the difference between the social relationships of the proletariat and those of the bourgeoisie, and the amount of self-determination each class has. Economic security provides freedom from responsibility, from the need to rely on neighbours, from exigencies of fate and from the consequences of actions.

> The class above her, living in security, can afford to hold the outer world at arm's length. Those who belong to it are rarely dependent for their interests, their entertainment, or their livelihood upon chance encounters. They are making their way through a realm that is policed and protected at every turn; and the fear of chaos, of disaster, is remote from their minds. The poor, on the other hand, cannot afford to hold potential friends at a distance. (HM, p.86)

There is an awareness of how class difference affects access to power in *No Mean City*. The characters articulate the belief that power and control are the domain of the ruling class, whose property the corrupt police exist to protect. Slum dwellers fear and mistrust the 'polis' and do not turn to them for help.

The only possibility for individual agency and empowerment for young working class men within this environment is to join a gang. So the novel provides an insight into why gangs exist, bred from poverty and deprivation, gang psychology supplying a sense of belonging in the midst of alienation, providing peer-group approval and local fame for the fiercest.

In *No Mean City* there is a desperate desire of the characters to escape from the Gorbals and improve the material conditions of their existence – 'to better themselves'.[15] Lily and Bobby succeed in achieving some of their social ambitions through their rising careers

---

15 Not to be confused with what this novel refers to as 'The Escape Complex' or avoidance behaviour discussed later in this chapter.

as dancing instructors and depart the Gorbals for a while. But by the end of the novel they are forced back to the old neighbourhood, crushed by poverty and powerlessness. Their desire to escape needs to be more than just aspirational for it to be effective, but they are trapped by social conditioning. Peter Stark, Johnnie's brother, is also ambitious, believing in the myth of meritocracy, of the possibility of his personal power to overcome the restrictions of his environment. As a 'messenger boy' he imagines that with brains and hard work he can climb his way up to being a 'traveller' (travelling salesman) and eventually a 'sales manager'. (NMC, p.72) However his ambitions are also stunted by life in the Gorbals and conditioned into believing:: 'he never fooled himself that he would be able to set up in business on his own account…That he should become an employer and a capitalist was a dream simply beyond the range of his imagination.' (NMC, p.72) Eventually even Peter's limited hopes are thwarted by the Depression and unemployment. The subtext of *No Mean City* is that it is not possible to transcend class difference; degradation and poverty are not a matter of choice but of social conditioning and economic limitation. Peter thinks that his family would not be bothered if he, 'never escaped at all from the dreary contentment of mass failure'. (NMC, p.72) But his brother, Johnnie the Razor King, has a more realistic and accurate assessment of how difficult it is to escape the poverty trap, and scorns the false consciousness of those who think they can better themselves. In an insightful passage detailing the futility of working class ambitions in the face of a fickle and indifferent capitalist system, Johnnie warns his brother of injustice and the impossibility of change and the inevitability of failure for his kind:

> I've seen your kind before – plenty of them, likely fellas, goin' to toil every day, kissin' the boss's backside when he throws them a good word; readin' books and newspapers; …dead sure, every one of them, that they're going to get on in the world….What happens to them aw? They get married and they have kids. An' the wages doesny grow with the family. An they take to drink a little later instead of sooner. An' the shop shuts or the yard shuts down or there's a bliddy strike. An' there they go, back to the dung heap, haudin' up the street corners, drawin' their money from the parish, an' keepin' awa oot of the hoose all day, awa frae the auld wife's tongue and the kids that go crawlin' and messin' aroon the floor." (NMC, p.113)

'The escape complex' articulated in *Hunger March* is more geographical than hierarchical in its aspiration. Joe dreams of escaping the city of Glasgow altogether, of emigrating from Scotland to a new country: 'America, India, Canada ...Oh to leave behind all the hopelessness, the mess; to start afresh in a new country!'(HM, p.72) However he too eventually succumbs to the realisation that there is no escape from the oppressive, poverty stricken conditions of life in Glasgow, not even by emigrating, as the novel describes how many of those who did escape this way were forced to return home due to the global economic crisis of the 1930s.

The ability to escape class destiny appears to be one of the differences between *Major Operation* and *No Mean City* on the one hand; and *The Shipbuilders*, and *Gael Over Glasgow* on the other. The denouement of *Gael Over Glasgow* has the setting up of an imaginary utopia to which Brian O'Neill can escape from the poverty of unemployment in a Clydeside where there is no work, but one which in its nature and scope is entrepreneurial; while Danny Shields the unemployed shipyard worker in *The Shipbuilders*, also becomes an entrepreneur with his own small business at the end of the novel. However in *No Mean City* the only opportunities presented for escape from the class trap are prison, 'the madhouse', or death. (NMC, p.32); and *Major Operation*, despite all its Marxist revolutionary rhetoric, has an overarching tone imbued with existential futility, fatalism and the inevitability of death, viewed as 'the eternal contradiction of life: in the Second City as elsewhere', (MO, p.117) and the only character who does escape his pre-determined class fate, George Anderson the bourgeois business man turned unemployed revolutionary, is literally trampled to death at the end of the novel. There are no grounds for optimism here.

Conclusion

The five realist novels all document the alienation and anomie in inter-war Glasgow: a condition that can come about in societies undergoing sudden economic change, and when there is a discrepancy between commonly professed values and what is actually achievable in reality. In the novels the disaffected underclass are shown escaping from intolerable social conditions in the pub, gambling, football or gang violence; the vices are mixed but alcohol is often a factor. Together with sectarian and workplace divisions and the illusory allure of upward social mobility, this creates an unstable combination contributing to mass false consciousness and acting as a possible deterrent to revolutionary action. Although a major message of all the novels is the idea that in labour lies sovereignty and empowerment; a counterpoint is that they present most of their protagonists as fated for failure, trapped and determined by their class position and the economic situation - the one exception in *Gael Over Glasgow* has a somewhat improbably positive conclusion. Thus whatever possibility for social change the novels may have been attempting to convey, their subtexts subvert any potential for human agency in the transformation of social conditions.

6   Liminal City

Literary and Historical Evaluation

The inter-war era was a defining moment in the history of Glasgow and in the narrative of the city. More than seventy years onwards it has been revealing to look at the ways in which the city was depicted textually in the five realist Glasgow novels from the 1930s; and to examine their realism by comparison with contemporary non-fictional representations. It has been argued here that Glasgow's more recent history can be understood in terms of the lasting effects of the inter-war period on the economic and social life of the city; and that the five novels map out the effects of the Great Depression on inter-war Glasgow, bearing testament to a liminal moment in the history of the city.

The realist novels have value and validity as both historical and literary documents: certain patterns permeate serving to support such an assertion and contributing towards the myth of revolutionary Glasgow. All the writers filter the politics of the time through varying degrees of class-consciousness in a style that is generally journalistic. Although not all the novels can be judged as successful products of 'social' realism, the defining features of which are political and social commitment combined with an alternative vision of the future, all the texts record an historical era in ways which do realistically correspond to non-fictional representations from the time. Therefore they can be judged as satisfactory realism, and useful historical documents in and of themselves. It is anomalous given the ongoing emphasis in Glasgow on the legend of Red Clydeside and the heroes of the time, and the numinous quality this era has assumed in the consciousness of the city, that the very novels which document this so realistically should have drifted into obscurity. A question that needs to be asked is: why then did the former Second City of Empire, and the novels that represent it so realistically during the inter-war era, enter into a state of lingering liminality?

Renaissance Glasgow — Literary Evaluation

There is little (surviving) literary criticism from the inter-war era pertaining to the five realistic Glasgow novels. Throughout the period literary critics continued to lament the lack of an epic novel to represent the life of Scotland, indicating a failure to take into account the realist novels already published. Three of these novels did fulfill the epic role: *Major Operation*, *The Shipbuilders*, and *Gael Over Glasgow*; as too did the component parts of Lewis Grassic Gibbon's *A Scots Quair* already published in 1934.[1]

In a survey of the historical development of the novel in Scotland (1978) encompassing fifty novelists and over two hundred Scottish novels, Francis Russell Hart finds that, 'The Scottish novel suffers from a passive conspiracy of neglect'.[2] However he himself then proceeds to neglect the existence of most of the Glasgow inter-war realist novels: perhaps because they were difficult to source. Hart himself admits that his survey of the Scottish novel is 'lamentably incomplete', suggesting the reason for this as being the 'unavailability of many of the novels'.[3] His survey discusses only one of the inter-war realist novels *The Shipbuilders*, which he cites as an expression of the Scottish epic together with Gibbon's *A Scots Quair*.[4] It is perplexing that Hart overlooks *Major Operation* and *Gael Over Glasgow*, yet both of these novels seem to comply with his definition of an epic:

> The epic novel of modern Scotland was to project a new ideology of national survival and at the same time demythologise a past that had become a force of romantic betrayal. Each demanded a protagonist with strong roots in a national past who could still present an admirable, viable identity in the face of a hostile, depersonalised modern world.[5]

Prevailing socio-economic conditions produced a particular form of literary representation of Glasgow during the inter-war years. A new genre of urban realist novels in Scottish literature came into being, as did the Condition of Scotland discourse. Both of these genres

---

1   Lewis Grassic Gibbon, *A Scots Quair* (Hutchinson & Co: London, 1946, repr. 1971).
2   Francis Russell Hart, *The Scottish Novel from Smollett to Spark* (Cambridge Massachusetts: Harvard University Press, 1978), p.viii-x.
3   Hart, Ibid. p.viii-x.
4   Hart, Ibid. p.213.
5   Hart, Ibid. p.215.

could have been considered a manifestation of the Scottish Cultural Renaissance taking place at the time. Oddly enough however, the novelists of inter-war Scotland encountered hostile skepticism from the Scottish Renaissance establishment. Hart reveals that:

> MacDiarmid often expressed the view that the novel is an inherently inferior form ... Edwin Muir saw the lack of vitality in the novel as an index of disbelief in Scottish society. In 1935, Linklater endorsed this unhappy diagnosis.[6]

Muir suggested in relation to the 1930's Glasgow novelists that: 'When people no longer believe very strongly in a society they cannot believe very strongly in representations of it either'. Eric Linklater judged *The Shipbuilders* a failure for the same reason, because he considered George Blake talented at 'painting epic panorama' when he 'writes of the Clyde itself, with its empty yards and its world-pacing history he is magnificent'. But Linklater goes on to argue that Blake sentimentalised his main characters beyond plausibility: 'He is not able to believe very strongly in the specific importance of Clyde shipbuilders, their wives, and their conservative employees, and therefore he has not given his representation of them sufficient force'.[7] Hart remarks wryly how in *The Shipbuilders* the narrator is, 'divided in the presence of the tragic pageant of the once-glorious Clyde', but Hart is sceptical of the truth of this interpretation enquiring: 'Was the glory ever real ... was the truth a tale of brief, brutal capitalist warfare leading to exploitation and collapse'?[8]

Blake himself, in a later mea culpa moment, admitted to an 'insufficient knowledge of working class life', and to the adoption of 'a middle class attitude to the theme of industrial conflict and despair'.[9] However the demise of the Clyde Shipbuilding era is actually presented with great pathos in *The Shipbuilders*, and it was possibly a genuine sense of loss that lead Blake and the other inter-war novelists into the passages of nostalgia and sentimentality that flaw their attempts at objective realism. Both sentiment and nostalgia serve to simplify the features of the object described,

---

6 Hart, Ibid p.207.
7 Eric Linklater, 'The Novel in Scotland', *Fortnightly Review* (Nov 1935), p. 621-624.
8 Hart, *The Scottish Novel from Smollett to Spark*, p.217.
9 George Blake, BBC Interview 1950, quoted in Hart, *The Scottish Novel from Smollett to Spark*. p213.

whether it be a worker or 'The Workers', and are more appropriate to features of idealism than realism. Therefore evidence of this must be regarded as a fault-line within realist texts. Sentiment creates a one-dimensional effect; nostalgia oversimplifies the relationship with current preoccupations, it has a selective memory retaining those features of the past corresponding to a present ideal that is no longer attainable.

A progressive attempt towards realism conflicts with a more backward looking impulse towards romantic idealism in all the inter-war Glasgow novels – the very Kailyard flaw they were projected to reject. Many of the inconsistencies in their realism spring from this slide towards idealism, and a glossing over of the inherent contradictions of real life. Jack Mitchell argues that this was a problem with many attempts at social realism of the time. While he hails *Major Operation* as the only one of the five novels considered here that fits the rubric of the 'genuine working class novel in Scotland',[10] Mitchell then criticizes Barke's characters as lacking any real conflict or contradiction, so that his novel: 'ultimately fails at the aesthetic level to provide an answer to no-mean-cityism'.[11] As a reason for this Mitchell posits the following argument which is worth quoting in its entirety as it is pertinent to the analysis of all the inter-war realist novels and their writers presented here:

> Disgusted with the corruption and ineptness of the ruling class and intoxicated with the first superficial draught of historical materialism, many left intellectuals romanticised the workers and then embraced their own romantic creation. Their attitude had more of moral idealism than historical materialism. The proletariat is seen not so much as a historicised developing class but rather as an absolute and therefore dehistoricised moral category whose superiority over the bourgeoisie lies in its moral excellence and lack of that inner conflict which ham-strings the middle class and its intellectuals. In fact it was a kind of escape into the state of "conflictlessness", a tempting wish-dream for intellectuals.[12]

The combination of idealism with realism in the novels cannot merely be dismissed as an expression of the oft discussed

---

10   Jack Mitchell, 'The struggle for the working class novel in Scotland', *Scottish Marxist* Part III No 8 January 1975. p.42.

11   Mitchell, Ibid. p.44.

12   Mitchell, Ibid. p.44.

contradictory impulses in Scottish literature. These supposed opposing literary tendencies indicating a perceived contrariness in the Scottish character, were first identified in print by literary critic G. Gregory Smith[13] in 1919 as: 'The Caledonian Antisyzygy ... almost a zigzag of contradictions ... an antithesis ... a combination of opposites ... a reflection of the contrasts which the Scot shows at every turn'.[14] Smith delineated what he considered to be two basic trends in Scottish literature: the impulse towards realism, facts and logic, evident in a persistent, 'zest for handling a multitude of details rather than for seeking broad effects by suggestion'; alongside an impulse towards fantasy, sentiment, superstition and romance, which he defines as the 'polar twins of the Scottish Muse'.[15] John Buchan extrapolated on this idea by proposing, 'two master elements in the Scottish character, hard-headedness on the one hand and romance on the other: common sense and sentiment: practicality and poetry: business and idealism', adding that 'the peculiarity of the Scottish race is that it has both in a high degree'.[16] The concept of Antisyzygy was taken up by writers and critics, most famously by Hugh MacDiarmid, but also by Edwin Muir who argued it was a negative trend in Scottish literature.[17] However the contention can be made that this romance/realism paradox is not exclusively Scottish, but a component characteristic of humanity, torn between the tug of sentiment and reason, a trait that is evident in the writers of all cultures and in much of so-called realism everywhere.

Roderick Watson argues that a belief in archetypal values is evident in the work of Edwin Muir, Lewis Grassic Gibbon, Neil Gunn and George Mackay Brown who, 'could be said to form a distinctively Scottish school of mythopoeic realism whose origins go back to these earlier movements in anthropology and the "Celtic" ideal'.[18]

---

13 Although this is an idea sometimes erroneously attributed to Hugh MacDiarmid.

14 G. Gregory Smith, *Scottish Literature: Character and Influence*. (Macmillan & Co: London, 1919), p.3-5,

15 Smith. Ibid pp.19-20.

16 John Buchan, 'Some Scottish Characteristics', in *The Scottish Tongue*, ed. by W.A.Craigie, John Buchan, Peter Giles and J.M. Bulloch (Cassell & Company: London, 1924), p.58.

17 Muir argued that the existence of the Scots language is proof that Scottish consciousness is divided as the Scots feel in the Scottish tongue, and think in standard English, which results in a separation between emotion (poetry) and intellect (prose). Edwin Muir, 'Language', in *Scott and Scotland: The Predicament of the Scottish Writer* (Routledge: London, 1936), pp.17-22.

18 Roderick Watson, *The Literature of Scotland*. (London: MacMillan, 1984) p.313

Although Watson does not mention them, certain aspects of the inter-war novels fit into this category, most markedly *Gael Over Glasgow*. However it could possibly be regarded as a denial of modernity to postulate Scottish identity in the early twentieth century as comprised of a lingering synthesis of the pragmatic Presbyterian work ethic originating from the Scottish lowlands, with an older pre-industrial Celtic Catholic mysticism (often incorrectly) associated with the highlands.

Possibly the most interesting contribution of the proletarian novels lies in their observation of Glasgow in the 1920s and 1930s; their realistic representation of the everyday life of the city at a time of great social change and upheaval; and their portrayal of the effects of the Great Depression on the Glasgow population. In this study non-fictional representations of the city that correspond with the depiction of events and situations in the novels have been sourced for comparison and verification of the realism. The findings are that, in this respect, the five novels are expressions of social realism, differing from the dominant tradition in fiction of the early twentieth century – the self-absorption of the Modernist novel with its placing of the individual subject at the centre of the work — in that they emphasise the concerns of the wider society and contain objective descriptions of social and economic realities.

Three of the novelists were journalists, and the style of all the novels could be described as journalistic, written as social commentary and exposé with an intention to convince their audience. Edwin Morgan predicted that Blake was 'likely to endure rather as an acute social commentator and historian than as a novelist',[19] and this judgement could be applied to all five of the inter-war realist novelists discussed here. Grassic Gibbon avers that Barke is at his best when writing about Glasgow, 'dealing with life in that deplorable city, the vomit of a cataleptic commercialism'. However in an ironic review of an earlier novel of Barke's, the spirit of which can also be applied to Barke's later later novel *Major Operation*, Gibbon describes Barke's writing style in terms of its strengths: 'all the Scots virtues and most of the faults; he is apt, acute and passionate', and weaknesses: 'And he preaches and proses and halts through long stretches to tell the bored reader, over and over again, just how his hero felt and considered

---

19 Edwin Morgan, 'Who will publish Scottish poetry', *New Saltire*, No 2, Nov 1961, pp. 51-56.

and was spiritually uplifted and spiritually tormented.'[20]   It is true that an overly conscientious attention to detail is a tedious feature of all five of the realistic inter-war novels. Detailed descriptions can be a signifier of successful realism, although an aspect that can slither too easily into naturalism — a characteristic which Georges Lukács argues distinguishes much of modernist literature.

In contrast to naturalism, Lukács defines realism as utilising devices such as the historically typical character and action, and as being both representative and prophetic.[21]   The inter-war realist novels are not necessarily prophetic of future possibilities, but they are representative of typical Glaswegian characters and the life of the city during a particular moment in history. Blake's realism is commended by Linklater: 'he can find abundant riches in crowded places or in a small domestic atmosphere'.[22] Douglas Gifford avers that an expression of the legacy of the 'Democratic Intellect' in Scotland is evident in 'all the unpretentious and unglamorous protagonists whose role in countless Scottish novels is to be the ordinary member of community',[23] a reference to the historical legacy of the Reformation and the Scottish Enlightenment and the influence on Scots writers. Hugh MacDiarmid (as himself C.M. Grieve) refers to this tradition when describing Barke:

> He was one of the all too few Scottish writers of his generation who made the same choice that all the great line of Scottish radical writers have made, ...who sided with the working class and lived and wrote for the Social Commonwealth... animated by the cause of Social Justice.[24]

Lukács' discussion of social realism posits that literature will be the truest mirror of reality if it fully reflects the contradictions of social development, and demonstrates insights into the structure of society and the future direction of its evolution.[25] Therefore if social

20 Lewis Grassic Gibbon, 'Scots Novels of the Half Year', *Free Man* 2:21, 24 June 1933, p.7.
21 Georges Lukács, *Realism in Our Time,* (New York: Harper & Row, 1964) p.20
22 Linklater, 'The Novel in Scotland', pp.621-624.
23 Douglas Gifford and others, eds. *Scottish Literature* (Edinburgh University Press: Edinburgh 2002), p.234.
24 Christopher Murray Grieve's speech at New Kilpatrick Cemetery, Bearsden at the committal service of James Barke, Author, 24 March 1958 – taken from the copy in Box 10 of the Barke Papers in the Mitchell Library Glasgow.
25   Georges Lukács *Studies in European Realism*, (New York: Grosset & Dunlap, 1964) p.43.

realism is an attempt to describe life without idealism or romantic subjectivity then, as discussed earlier, there are certain aspects of all five inter-war novels that would fall short of this goal. It could be argued however that there is a contradiction inherent in social realism: progressive ideas are being presented in what is essentially a conservative genre.[26] On the socio-historical level the subject matter of the Glasgow inter-war proletarian novels is the discussion of radical disruption; on the literary level the medium of realism is the stable text, it is descriptive and it does not challenge. So in the five novels under discussion there is a stable form describing an unstable situation: a possible answer to the question of why these novels have not survived. A key characteristic of modernism was a disruption of this stability through a disintegrated text where the reader's vantage point was no longer fixed but challenged by the text itself. For example *Scottish Scene* by Gibbon and MacDiarmid is a deliberately disruptive contradictory mix of genres.[27] Terry Eagleton argues that the realist novel is actually 'reformist in spirit' and suggests that realism in the sense of 'verisimilitude' (the semblance of truth) is not necessarily revolutionary.[28]

It possible to posit that the inter-war realist novels are progressive neither in style nor content. In terms of content they are not a total departure from the Kailyard – as evidenced by their nostalgia and sentimentality, and they do not offer a strong political vision. Perhaps in both style and content they reflect the lack of sufficient movement to enable revolution against the dominant forces of the status quo. The novels are critical of the existing order of things, and they may have a sub-textual belief in the possibility of a different society, but they don't offer an alternative vision to what actually exists. The Glasgow inter-war realist novels are therefore diagnostic rather than remedial, delineating the problem rather than offering solutions to it, and thus do not offer up any realistic models for the salvation of society, other than a Rousseau type back-to-the-land utopia in *Gael Over Glasgow*, and an undefined possibility of revolutionary transformation in *Major Operation*.[29] As Eagleton suggests, when he

---

26 Alan Riach, Pers. comm. University of Glasgow, May 2009.

27 Lewis Grassic Gibbon and Hugh MacDiarmid, *Scottish Scene or The Intelligent Man's Guide to Albyn* (Cedric Chivers: Bath, 1934, repr.1974).

28 Terry Eagleton, *The English Novel: An Introduction* (Blackwell: Oxford, 2005) p.7

29 Both these possibilities synthesised in Gibbon's vision in *Scots Quair* at the end of *Sunset Song* when after the socio-economic changes of WW1 Chris returns

augments Lukács's theory of realism with that of Marx and Engels' Principle of Contradiction, 'the political views of an author may run counter to what his work objectively reveals'.[30]

Subsequent analysis of any realist text may lead to readings against the grain as any work is 're-authored' by the socio-economic, geographic, political and historical stance of the reader. As with most textual representations, the realistic Glasgow novels contain contradictions, gaps, silences and slippages. The novels tend to serve as a mouthpiece for the philosophy of their writers, and in doing so introduce the ethos of their era, some of which can be difficult for the reader to access in the twenty-first century. This includes a narrative posture of skeptical humour which reveals particular anachronistic prejudices. Gifford claims that 'The Scottish novel was by the mid-1930s increasingly extending its perspective of ironic social realism to the city.'[31] However the five inter-war novels hold inconsistencies within their ironic stance and contradictions within their project. This may be a result of an inherent ambivalence in the writers' subject position. The novels critique the capitalist system while identifying with middle class values. They are fundamentally flawed by the prejudices of the time, for example misogyny, and racism against 'dagos', 'yids', and 'coolies'. Different ethnic groups and women are written into the texts as some form of inferior, 'othered' class, a stance that does not wear well historically. They do not mention disability in what was a notoriously disabling working and living environment.[32] They are all silent on homosexuality, although *Gael Over Glasgow* contains lyrical passages of sublimated homo-erotic longing, the emotional male-bonding between the opposing class protagonists in *The Shipbuilders* and *Major Operation* are perhaps more of the same, and there is an element of this in the gang culture of Johnnie and his boys in *No Mean City*. All the novels contain evidence of the inevitable sectarianism endemic to Glasgow, though not necessarily at a critical remove.

Women historically played a significant role in the political <u>struggles of inter-war Glasgow, but the images of Red Cly</u>deside

to the land while her son the young radical Ewan sets off on a protest march to London.

30 Eagleton, Ibid, p.57

31 Douglas Gifford, *Scottish Literature*, p.716.

32 For descriptions of the effects of lack of health and safety precautions in Glasgow industry see Ralph Glasser, *Growing up in the Gorbals*, (Edinburgh: Black & White Publishing, 2006)

are mostly male, and the eulogized aspects of Glasgow's industrial past revolve around the male-dominated industries of shipbuilding and heavy engineering. This imbalance of gender representation is reflected in the novels. Four out of the five novels discussed here are written by men, although this could too glibly be regarded as a reason why their depiction of female characters is uniformly one-dimensional. Neil McMillan argues this is a phenomenon that continues today within a tradition of male Glasgow fiction that, 'persistently identifies womanliness with negative bourgeois aspirations',[33] a trend evident in the inter-war novels where the little visible presence accorded to women allocates them just such conservative, middle class pretensions.[34] The elitist attitudes of most of the women characters in the novels may be ciphers for a reactionary element of Glasgow's middle classes at the time. A possible speculation is that if the characters in the novels were drawn from life, and if this mind-set was prevalent in Glasgow, it would have acted as a deterrent on any movement towards social change.

All the novels contain a sub-text of the irrelevance of individual struggles against larger class interests, in some cases contradicting their obvious intention to the contrary. Despite their circumstances, many of the characters in the novels are aspirational, not just in terms of political will, but in their desire to better their standing within the class system, to move from the working class to the middle class, thus displaying an ambition not so much to subvert the upper classes but to emulate them. In *The Shipbuilders* and *No Mean City* the narrative conveys a lack of awareness of the true nature of class-relationships, an acceptance of unequal power relationships, and a sense of the powerlessness of the individual to act as a subjective agent against the determinist forces of the capitalist state. These two novels could thus be seen to reflect false consciousness and a reinforcement of the status quo, even if this was not the intentional project of their writers. The novels all do in fact appear to have been written from a determinist position which begs the question of the ability of the individual to act freely. All the characters are bound up in a dance over which they have no control and the right to protest in the novels is more of a predicament than an empowerment. If this

---

33 Neil McMillan, 'Wilting or the "Poor Wee Boy Syndrome", Kelman and Masculinity', in *Edinburgh Review* No.108, p.49.

34 A notable exception to this is the positive portrayal of Jock MacKelvie's wife in *Major Operation* as a strong, supportive working class woman.

sense of helplessness was external to the novels then perhaps it could go some way to explaining why revolutionary change in Glasgow remained incomplete. However it could also be that the writers of the realist novels, being as they were (mostly) white, liberal, middle class Scottish intellectuals, as such were out of touch with the true temper of working class consciousness in the city.

The determinism of the inter-war novels may reflect an inherent conservatism, not allowing much space for the agency of the individual, freedom of choice or escape from oppressive social conditions. They document lives enslaved by poverty, low wages, drink and violence, and so also contain an ethos of existential tragedy inherent in their project. The novels, to a greater or lesser degree, chart their protagonists' journey towards a point of political realisation, even if that realisation is one of impotence. This could indicate an acceptance of the status quo and thus resignation, and so be another deterrent to action or revolution. The characters in the novels, in most instances, seem to be destined to failure. There is a grim inevitability in Johnnie's progression towards his demise in *No Mean City*, while only a miracle could save Pagan's shipyard in *The Shipbuilders*. In fact it is only a miracle that enables *Gael Over Glasgow* to end on a positive note, as being rescued by a long lost, benevolent, rich uncle in 1930s Glasgow was probably not an everyday occurrence. The title of *Hunger March* is misleading as it does not posit the Unemployed Workers Movement and the hunger marches of the 1930s at the centre of the narrative, or revolution as a real possibility. *Major Operation* is the most deserving of the sobriquet 'social realism', as is evident in the conclusion that suggests the possibility of impending revolution. In the final lines of this novel, in his funeral oration for George, Jock the worker leader quotes from the Communist Manifesto regarding the best representatives of the bourgeois class defecting to the proletariat – so providing a vaguely hopeful possibility of future social transformation.

Who was the intended audience for the realist novels? Were they written for the bourgeoisie as social documentation, or was their creation an act of indignation? Are they intended as historical witnesses and testaments to the reconstruction of an era? Jack Mitchell argues that Barke was writing for intellectuals in that he places the ideological battle at the centre of the narrative in *Major Operation*, with the hospital ward set up as 'clinical debating chamber ... Such an emphasis was geared to interest and win over the potential intellectual ally'.[35] The uneven tone of *No Mean City* is interspersed with a patronising narrative voice indicating it is addressing a middle class audience. Contemporary Glaswegians must have read, and possibly identified with, the images presented in the realistic novels during the inter-war years, perhaps recognising themselves reflected in the characters. However as discussed earlier, the characters in the five novels tend to be one-dimensional, each the mere embodiment of an idea, demonstrating a weakening of realism, a slide into idealism, and a limitation of the possibilities of the characters. Characters in a novel only become believable when portrayed with complexity and difference, light and dark, competence and error, ability and fallibility, contradiction and paradox. However this is not always evident in the Glasgow inter-war realist novels.

Dystopian views of the industrialised city were not new, but after the idealised depictions of the city that occurred with the Scottish Urban Kailyard, the realistic inter-war novels were the first reflections of the truth of Glasgow's industrialised dark side. The novels can be read as a realistic manifestation of the zeitgeist of the Great Depression: in order to realistically represent the era, the proletarian novels of inter-war Clydeside had to be pessimistic, gritty, and dark. It can be averred that these novels set up the conceit of Glasgow as 'Prolier than thou', an imagery for future representations of the city: the breadlines and the violence and the dole, illustrating failure in the workplace and the world. They also provided the basis for the proletarian novels of Glasgow that came later in the twentieth century. Gifford discusses how *The Shipbuilders* ran counter to the dominant trend of the time which celebrated Clyde mythology: 'George Blake favours an elegiac strain which prefigures Clyde mythology as doomed ...in a manner prophetic of a major strand of modern Scottish fiction, which continues to the present.'[36]

The work of the inter-war novelists accurately reflects the reality and expresses the alienation of the time. What is to be done is to recognise the significance of the novels as historical documentations of the era, and a literary basis for a new genre in the narrative of Glasgow. What is required is a re-evaluation of the realistic novels of inter-war Glasgow, to provide a recovered understanding of the past from whence the present of the city evolved. Perhaps the crucial

35 Mitchell, 'The struggle for the working class novel in Scotland'. p.43.
36 Douglas Gifford and others, eds. *Scottish Literature*, p.717.

literary proposal to be made about the Glasgow inter-war novels is that as a formal procedure realism may not be adequate. More was needed, a leap of imaginative faith; one taken later in what became known as 'The Monumental Glasgow Novels': by Archie Hind in *Dear Green Place*, Alasdair Gray in *Lanark*, William McIlvanney in *Laidlaw*, James Kelman in *How Late it was How Late*.[37] The possible significance of the inter-war novels is that they provided a creative springboard for these later novels with Glasgow as their theme and setting.

Revolutionary Glasgow — Historical Evaluation

The economic context in which the creation of the realistic novels of Clydeside took place was the crisis in world capitalism during the inter-war period, particularly devastating to Scotland and the heavily industrialised area of Glasgow. Because the emphasis in these novels is the effects of the economic crisis on the working class of Glasgow, the focus of the analysis has been on the political and revolutionary more than the cultural and renaissance aspects of the era.

The culture of Glasgow was created by its workers in the heavy manufacturing and shipbuilding industries that were so intrinsic to the development and identity of the city. It was nurtured in the working class neighbourhoods surrounding the industrial areas; in the streets, the closes and the tenements of the city. Glaswegian culture flourished because of, and despite, some of the harshest working and social conditions in the world, it grew out of unemployment, poverty, exploitation, bad housing, overcrowding, alcoholism, social squalor, and all the human alienation and anomie of the industrial revolution.[38] This awareness permeates with great poignancy the realistic Glasgow novels published during the 1930s. Thus these novels serve as a documentation of social conditions of the period, conditions which continue in many parts of the city seven decades later, despite the economic circumstances that gave rise to them having long since disappeared.

The influence of Scottish Presbyterianism has had both positive and negative effects on the culture of Glasgow. The democratic, egalitarian traditions of the Kirk influenced Glasgow's history of trade unionism and socialism. Many of the Glasgow socialist leaders

---

37 Alan Riach, Pers. comm. University of Glasgow, March 2009.
38 Discussed by Seán Damer, *Glasgow — Going for a Song* (Lawrence & Wishart Ltd: London,1990).

of the inter-war labour movement were atheist, but had religious roots that emerged in the strong ethical and moral idealism of the movement. They fervently believed in the ideal of improving the living and working conditions of their people. John Grierson, the Scots film documentary-maker of the 1930s, argued that, 'at the heart of our national philosophy' is an 'obligation to work and aspire for the common good'.[39] However the rhetoric of equality in Scotland was, and still is, undermined by the reality of a deeply embedded social stratification at all levels. In Glasgow industry a history of job protectionism and hierarchical organisation of the workforce, with Protestants as the labour elite in some of the more traditional industries, was a response to the influx of Catholic Irish into the region during the nineteenth and early twentieth centuries. These old sectarian divisions and prejudices are still to be found in the city, an unusual anachronism in what is, in many other respects, a subtle and sophisticated society.

Scotland, and most particularly Glasgow, provided many of the ideas and inventions in the eighteenth and nineteenth centuries that facilitated the industrial revolution and the development of capitalism. However, during the twentieth-century Glasgow became known as a city with a dependency culture. The proletarian novels of the inter-war era all have as their unifying theme the enervating effect of unemployment on the skills and morale of the working class. The loss of the highly skilled craftsmen and artisans of Clydeside can never be regained. It is possible to argue as did George Malcolm Thomson, that emigration was what deprived Scotland of its potential leaders and entrepreneurs: 'the drain of the educated, intelligent, and energetic middle class youth who would normally become the leaders of the commercial, political and intellectual life of the country.'[40] This 'brain-drain' provided much energy to the Scottish Diaspora and enhanced the reputation abroad of the Scots for being an entrepreneurial nation.[41]

---

39 John Grierson, *The Salt of the Earth, John Grierson's Scotland*, ed. by Forsyth Hardy (The Ramsay Head Press: Edinburgh, 1979), p.32.

40 George Malcolm Thomson, *Caledonia or the Future of the Scots* (Kegan Paul: London 1927), pp. 47-51.

41 Arthur Herman attributes the undermining of entrepreneurial spirit in Scotland to the co-option and corruption of the Scots ruling classes by English values, and an obsession with bourgeois respectability which stifled innovation and creativity. Arthur Herman, *The Scottish Enlightenment: The Scots Invention of the Modern World* (Fourth Estate: London, 2002), pp.349-353.

The efforts during the 1930s to revive and regenerate the inter-war economy culminated in the Glasgow Empire Exhibition of 1938, just before the start of the Second World War. This was a marketing device for Scottish enterprise, a display and celebration of a British Empire that would only last another four years, destined to destruction by a Nazi Empire designed to last a thousand years. The reported reaction of Glaswegians who attended the 1938 Exhibition was their overwhelming impression of contrast: between the possibilities of the brave new modernist world portrayed by the exhibition and the grimy Glasgow of the inter-war era; their wonder at the profligate water wastage from the numerous exhibition fountains compared with the 'one tap in the kitchen' home in which the majority lived; and the fantasy contrast of the whitewashed exhibition buildings as opposed to the blackened tenement buildings of Glasgow in the 1930s.[42] With hindsight it is possible to acknowledge that the 1938 Exhibition was made possible only owing to the skilled manpower available from the shipbuilding industry in Glasgow at the time. The construction of the pre-fabricated Exhibition buildings was a transferable skill from the fitment workshops of the shipyards, expertise that was lost, along with the possibility of its relocation to other industries, when the shipyards closed.

The ongoing class struggle is evident in all the novels, and the political and industrial action specific to the inter-war era is represented in *Gael Over Glasgow*, *Major Operation* and *Hunger March*. This class struggle may not have led to revolution, but could be posited as being a contributing factor to Glasgow's demise as an industrial powerhouse. It has been argued elsewhere that the uncompromising attitude of the Clydeside trade unions contributed to the dissolution of the region's economy. On the other side of the class divide, the owners of the means of production were possibly more preoccupied with the potential danger posed by a rebellious workforce than that of dwindling orders and the need to transform technology, this at a time when other nations were moving towards different labour practices and modern manufacturing techniques.[43]

---

42 In September 2008 the Glasgow Film Theatre (GFT) screened the Glasgow Digital Studio's recreation of the 1938 Exhibition along with documentary and home movie footage from the time. There was much interesting feedback from the audience, some of whom could recall attending the actual event.

43 The anomaly in the novels is the representation of the patrician shipyard owner Leslie Pagan who cares about his workers in *The Shipbuilders*.

Glasgow's continuing image as revolutionary city is mediated by contradictory forces. It is evident from the novels that the police and press were popularly perceived to uphold the interests of the property-owning classes. The myth of Red Clydeside seems to stem more from the echoes of these class struggles and the anxieties of the ruling elite in a volatile situation, than from any real threat of imminent insurrection at the time. There were three main periods of civil unrest during the inter-war era that unnerved the authorities in terms of the potential for revolution. Bloody Friday 1919 in George Square did happen, but evidence indicates it was caused by a massive over-reaction on the part of the media and the state, precipitated by the paranoia induced after the success of the Russian Revolution and Europe-wide industrial unrest. This is similar to the heavy handed reaction of the authorities to the General Strike of 1926, and the way in which the press and police ratcheted up the perceived threat of gang warfare in Glasgow and throughout Britain during the inter-war era. The advent of the Great Depression could only add to this unstable mélange. However the National Unemployed Workers Movement and the hunger marches of the 1930s were radical, but seemingly not revolutionary.

All three periods of civil unrest were instances of class warfare. However from the first hand accounts of those involved, it is evident that none evolved into revolutionary situations, nor were they intended to do so. One of the common denominators between 1919 and 1926 was the reaction of Winston Churchill, who in both instances fomented fear of Bolshevik inspired attempts to overthrow the government and so responded with a show of armed force. Ruling class fears concerning the 'Red' threat were answered with law abiding and peaceful demonstrations. It could also be argued that moderation stifled reform during the inter-war years, and that Britain, and even so-called radical Scotland, did not have the extremism necessary for revolution and never experienced the violent politics that fragmented Europe in the early twentieth century.

It is feasible that the very oppressive nature of social conditions deprived the unemployed of the will to organise into a revolutionary force in the 1930s, as evidenced in the descriptions in the novels of how their energy was exhausted by the very hunger they were marching against. Furthermore, alongside left-wing politics there were influences on Glasgow working class culture that were conservative and reactionary, emerging from religious sectarianism and a trade union movement historically concerned with job demarcation and protecting its own interests, all of which may have undermined a united front. Yet the myth of Red Clydeside continues to hold a numinous power over Glaswegians and outsiders alike, as John Foster avers:

> The vigour with which this episode has been contested and redefined, the sheer refusal of its ghost to disappear, bears witness to its continuing importance for the ways Scots define themselves today.[44]

An impression is gained from the realist novels, and the accounts of the Red Clydeside leaders, of a Glasgow inter-war population with a strong work ethic, whose related social ambitions left little opportunity or desire to overturn the existing order of things, even when they were unemployed. There is also indication of a complacency to dispute the use of excessive force by the authorities. The fear of losing their precarious social position may have mitigated against risk-taking behaviour in those who had jobs, however badly paid. This in addition to the fixed class-distinctions which appear in the novels, reveals a population in which people 'knew their place', and took pride in being part of the collective identity of the 'greatest shipbuilding city in the world' and 'Second City of the British Empire'. This credence in the dominant ideology would have precluded a critical awareness in the majority of the population regarding the material causes of their lived reality; or an acknowledgement of the inequities of the very social relations which exploited the working class and made exploiters of the bourgeoisie. George's act of sacrifice at the end of *Major Operation* could be regarded as a symbolic statement of the need for the leap of faith from safety into uncertainty, the necessary risking of security for revolution to occur.

There is a viewpoint which posits that social revolution needs to be rooted in the material conditions and radical ideology of the skilled working class. Sydney Checkland argues that this was not the case with the labour movement in Glasgow which, much like the rest of Britain, was not as affected by socialist ideas as were

---

44 John Foster, 'Red Clyde, Red Scotland'. in *The Manufacture of Scottish History*, eds. Ian Donnachie & Christopher Whatley, (Polygon: Edinburgh, 1992), p.108.

workers on the continent of industrialised Europe. He also posits that: 'there was relatively little response among the workers to the intellectualism of the radical middle class, or even those who like Maclean, had come from the working class, and little incentive to propound revolutionary solutions among themselves'.[45] Then there are revolutions, such as in 1917 Russia, that are led not so much by the workers as by a vanguard of bourgeois intellectuals. Many of the Scottish intelligentsia of the inter-war era were employing a sufficiently radical Marxist critique of prevailing socio-economic conditions, but possibly many of them were also too much involved in the cultural revolution of the Scottish Renaissance to contribute to the political activism necessary to achieve social revolution. There were exceptions, and evidence from their work indicates that both Gibbon and Muir, along with some of the writers of the realist novels and the Condition of Scotland texts, were concerned with ethical as well as aesthetic issues, denouncing the exploitative conditions of capitalism and the alienated value system advanced by bourgeois society. But it is uncertain how many intellectuals of the time were with them, and how this translated into political action. These are possibly questions for further investigation. It is one thing to articulate an understanding of reality, it is quite another to act upon it. Gibbon in *Scottish Scene* provides an impassioned insight into the tensions between ideology and practicality:

> There is nothing in culture or art that is worth the life and elementary happiness of one of those thousands who rot in the Glasgow Slums. There is nothing in science or religion. If it came (as it may come) to some fantastic choice between a free and independent Scotland, a centre of culture, a bright flame of artistic and scientific achievement, and providing elementary decencies of food and shelter to the submerged proletariat of Glasgow and Scotland. [46]

To speak of false consciousness being a deterrent to revolutionary force on the part of the proletariat, and the negated potential for vanguardism on the part of the bourgeoisie, is not to assume that the natural order of things is for an 'enlightened intelligentsia' to lead the way for a 'lumpenproletariat'. However it is to acknowledge

45 Sydney Checkland, *The Upas Tree: Glasgow 1875-1975* (University of Glasgow Press: Glasgow 1977), p.31.
46 Gibbon & MacDiarmid, *Scottish Scene*. p.141.

historical precedent, the restrictive nature of material conditions of existence, and the power of ideological hegemony. More importantly for this project, it is to reflect the reality of the material conditions in inter-war Glasgow represented in the novels under discussion.

Muir's concluding question at the end of the chapter entitled 'Glasgow' from *Scottish Journey* was this: 'The fundamental realities of Glasgow are economic. How is this collapsing city to be put on its feet again?'[47] This can perhaps best be answered with a quote from Gibbon's chapter entitled 'Glasgow' from *Scottish Scene*, in which he makes an appeal for an appreciation of diversity: 'Scotland's salvation, the world's salvation lies in neither nationalism nor internationalism, those twin halves of an idiot whole. It lies in ultimate cosmopolitanism'.[48] Glasgow society has never been homogenous, and now even more than then, may need to integrate an acceptance, rather than a judgment, of differences. Unfortunately a component aspect of the liminality of the city is the fixed quality of its prejudices, not obvious in its dominant ethos or the image it displays for public relations, but in the prevailing attitudes of certain sections of its population. The most mystifying aspect of reified social relations may be the inability of individuals to recognize the inhumanity of their own exploitation and the effect it has on their relationships with others. Instituted reification may be at the root of endemic social problems in Glasgow such as hate crime. Now, as averred by Gibbon during the inter-war era, a transformation is needed towards a culture in Glasgow that celebrates diversity and rejects the intolerance that has long divided the possibility for collective synergy within the city.

A post-colonial analysis may interpret divisions within Glasgow as a manifestation of the divide and rule strategy of British Imperialism, a complex project in which the Scots have played a role both as semi-subaltern and servitor-imperialist. In an attempt to find a solution to the problems of the nation during the inter-war period, MacDiarmid called for Scotland to resume an identity distinct from England. Complaining of the lack of political transparency or serious journalistic concern with Scottish affairs he argued, 'Less is known

---

47 Edwin Muir, *Scottish Journey* (Mainstream Publishing Company, Edinburgh, 1935, repr.1979), p.162.

48 Gibbon was possibly acknowledging the multi-ethnic nature of the Gorbals during the inter-war era (a lack in the narrative of *No Mean City*). Gibbon and MacDiarmid, *Scottish Scene*, p.146.

of the "powers behind the scenes" in Scotland – of the actualities of Scottish finance and ownership and control – than of any other country in Europe'.[49] His exposure of the infrastructure of Scotland as being set up by Westminster for military purposes, was what Alasdair Gray would denounce decades later in his novel *1982 Janine*: 'Scotland is wired for war, especially the bit north-west of Glasgow',[50] referring to the arsenal of nuclear submarines at the Faslane military base on the Firth of Clyde just west of the city. Despite Devolution in 1999, many of the same concerns persist, and the calls for an independent Scottish state continue.[51] Scotland may have regained a modicum of control over its own affairs, but the underlying issues of Scottish Nationalism remain the same as they were during the inter-war era: identity, and control over wealth and war.

Much has changed in Glasgow since the inter-war period, though much remains the same. During the twentieth century Glasgow was a place to leave, but in the twenty-first century it has become a place of return. There is a vast diaspora of descendents of those who emigrated from Scotland in the nineteenth and early twentieth centuries to the United States, Canada, Australia, many who now want to revisit their roots.[52] The Clyde was a working river well into the mid-twentieth century, but now all is quiet along the riverside where once echoed the pounding of riveters and the screech of machinery. The new generations in the city are economically detached from shipbuilding, although the industry continues to remain strong in living memory and in the mythology of the city. In the twenty-first century the problems of the city are more global than they were in the 1930s.

Glasgow is no longer the city of dreadful night. It has cleaned up its air, its buildings, streets, parks, housing and its image, though not always to the best effect. The need for breathing space and the ambition to transform and regenerate the city is a notion that runs throughout Glasgow's history. 'Liminal city' became 'possibility for elsewhere' as city planners attempted to rid the city of its claustrophobic slums through social engineering, resulting in a form of latter day Glasgow Clearances. The Gorbals and Govan, once

---

49 Gibbon and MacDiarmid, *Scottish Scene.* pp.39-41.
50 Alasdair Gray, *1982 Janine* (Jonathan Cape,: London, 1984), p.134.
51 In a survey by the Scottish Government Feb 2009, 75% of Scots identify themselves as Scottish rather than British (BBC news).
52 A phenomenon reflected in the increasing numbers of students from these regions who study Scottish History and Literature at the University of Glasgow.

busy working class residential areas and shipyard communities, today resemble a post-apocalyptic wasteland of empty demolition sites. The depressing image of crime and urban degeneration in the Gorbals, fostered by fiction and the media, was transformed in large part. But the crumbling, damp, tenement slums of the inner-city areas were replaced with crumbling, damp, high-rise apartment blocks on the margins of the city; dominating the Glasgow skyline like ironic incarnations of the possible power of the proletariat symbolised as monstrous in the inter-war novels.

Poverty and unemployment persist in Glasgow: they have merely been moved to the housing schemes and dormitory suburbs. These have become in their turn the focus of literature and media documentaries of urban deprivation in the liminal city. In response to a campaign advertising Glasgow as 'City of Culture' in 1990, Seán Damer posed the question: 'Glasgow Miles Better for Whom?'; and his answer was: 'not for the bulk of Glaswegians'.[53] Damer makes the important point that the superficial creation of an image for Glasgow can never reflect the real identity of the city rooted in its people, whose history of tough living and working conditions has securely fixed it as, 'the British industrial working class city par excellence'.[54] Glasgow twenty years later is now advertised as: 'Scotland with Style', and another question could be asked: Style for Whom? And the answer would still have to be: not for the majority of Glaswegians.

The significance of the inter-war era on the culture of the city is evident in the first decade of the twenty-first century. There is a plaque to John Maclean, the best known, perhaps most admired, of the Red Clydesiders, outside the concert hall in Candleriggs, describing him as a 'socialist pioneer who spoke here frequently to unemployed workers'. It overlooks four poems on the pavement below by Edwin Morgan commemorating the working people of Glasgow, one of which reads:

Ghostly workers sleep below
They hear no rain or heel and toe
Think of them where the forges glow
In the Glasgow of long ago.'[55]

---

53 Seán Damer, *Glasgow — Going for a Song*. p.13.
54 Damer, Ibid. p.209
55 Edwin Morgan, Poet Laureate of Glasgow, and in 2004 appointed first 'Scots Makar' or Poet Laureate of Scotland.

Alan Riach comments on the fact that these pavement poems are not overtly attributed to Morgan at the site: 'the anonymity says something about the way they work: their commemoration is of the people they name and suggest, more than their author.'[56] Riach reminds us of an important idea about literature, an idea that sometimes gets lost in the logic of critical analysis: the idea that 'Art makes long conversations possible with those who have gone.'[57] And it is these conversations with the dead, through the textual representations of a time long gone in the realistic novels of inter-war Glasgow, that can increase our understanding of the history and the city and its people. As we are now, so they once were.

Conclusion

Most of the inter-war realist novels of Clydeside were not readily available by the time Alasdair Gray made his famous pronouncement that Glasgow had only been the subject of a few bad novels and therefore did not feature in the literary imagination ... so possibly he was not referring to them.[58] It is difficult to discern the grounds for their neglect — the most obvious explanation today is that some have not been reprinted recently. Reasons for the disappearance of novels may lie in the changing marketing strategies of publishers, a history of reader reception, fashions in literary styles, and gate-keeping by literary critics and publicists. The identification and deconstruction of a canon of work, no matter how it may have been regarded previously, is a complex process. These novels are about events that are important. They are also literary artefacts that say something significant in themselves. Deciphering the texts is made all the more difficult as they were created within, and deal with, a particular shifting, liminal moment in the history of Glasgow: a city about which much has been said and a lot of it contradictory. Furthermore the sentimentalism of the novels and their lack of high literary merit may be a factor in their demise. Their time of first publication was also one when the focus was upon the Scottish Renaissance establishment and their projects, which may have marginalised others. The novels

---

56 Alan Riach, *Representing Scotland in Literature, Popular Culture and Iconography: The Masks of the Modern Nation* (Palgrave MacMIllan: Basingstoke, 2005),p.231.
57 Riach, Ibid.p.231
58 Alasdair Gray, *Lanark* (Palladin Books: London, 1981:1987) p. 243

could be interpreted as a basis for the later Monumental Novels of Glasgow, but it could be argued that the very success of the latter occluded the former. In fact the desire to purge the cultural scene of the Kailyard tendencies of sentimentality and nostalgia, some of which are evident in the inter-war realist novels, might have led to the condemnation of the literary merit of the works, discarding what is valuable with what is not. It is also possible that the nostalgic narrative of past industrial and shipbuilding glory and Glasgow hardmen found in these novels developed into a pastiche of itself: a new form of Kailyard sentimentality for a post-industrial world.

The crisis of capitalism during the inter-war era was a liminal historical moment for Glasgow, an economic, cultural and political threshold during which the city experienced: the transformation of global and local economy, the Scottish Cultural Renaissance, the revival of the Scots language, the rise of Scottish Nationalism, the emergence of new political influences, the upsurge of workers' movements, and the development of the city's revolutionary reputation. The five realist novels examined here were written in, represent, and themselves reflect the liminal condition of both Glasgow and its literature during the period between the two world wars. As a nascent attempt to move towards a more realistic urban genre they do not always succeed as idealism is still too evident, and this may be a contributing factor to their neglect. Although these inter-war novels did provide the foundation for realistic representations of Glasgow to develop successfully in fiction produced later in the twentieth century; the city itself has been seemingly incapable of making the transition required to flourish in a post-industrial age, remaining in a state of ongoing liminality for many of its inhabitants. But a limen is a place for passing through. The liminal should not become the label ... it cannot be the sticking place.

Bibliography

The five inter-war novels

ALLAN, Dot, *Hunger March,* (London: Hutchinson, 1934; repr. Glasgow: The Association for Scottish Literary Studies, 2010))

BARKE, James, *Major Operation,* (London: Collins, 1936, repr.1955)

BLAKE, George, *The Shipbuilders,* (Edinburgh: B&W Publishing, 1935, repr. 1993)

McARTHUR, Alexander and LONG, H.Kingsley, *No Mean City,* (London: Corgi Books, 1935, repr. 1998)

SHIELS, Edward, *Gael Over Glasgow,* (London: Sheed & Ward, 1937)

Primary sources from inter-war period

ABRAMS, M. *Home Market.* (London, 1937)

ALLAN, John R, *Scotland-1938 : Twenty-Five Impressions,* (Edinburgh: Oliver & Boyd,1938)

BLAKE, George, *The Heart of Scotland,* (London: Batesford, 1934)

BLAKE, George, *The Annals of Scotland 1895-1955,* (London: British Broadcasting Corporation, 1956)

BOARD OF TRADE, *An Industrial Survey of the South West of Scotland,* Political Economy Department of the University of Glasgow, (London: HMSO, 1932)

BOWIE, James, A., *The Future of Scotland: a Survey of the Present Position with Some Proposals for Future Policy,* (Edinburgh: W&R Chambers, 1939)

BOYD ORR, John, 'Scotland as it is' and 'Scotland as it might be', in Maclehose, Alexander, *The Scotland of our Sons,* (London: Alexander Maclehose, 1937)

BUCHAN, John, *Mr Standfast,* (Oxford University Press, 1919, repr.1993)

BUCHAN, John, 'Some Scottish Characteristics' in W.A. Craigie, John Buchan, Peter Giles & J.M. Bulloch, *The Scottish Tongue,* (London: Cassell & Company, 1924)

CARSWELL, Catherine, *Lying Awake,* (Edinburgh: Canongate, 1950, repr. 1997)

COCKBURN, John, 'The Scottish Novel: Can we uphold a renaissance that lacks the thing that matters?' *Scots Observer,* 25 February (1933), 9

GALLACHER, William, *Revolt on the Clyde,* (London: Lawrence & Wishart, 1936, repr.1990)

GIBB, Andrew, Dewar, *Scotland in Eclipse,* (London: Humphrey Toulmin, 1930)

GIBBON, Lewis, Grassic, 'Glasgow', *A Scots Hairst,* (London: Hutchinson, 1967, repr.1978) [First published in 1934 in *Scottish Scene,* Gibbon, Lewis Grassic and MacDiarmid, Hugh, (1934)]

GIBBON, Lewis, Grassic, *A Scots Quair,* (London: Hutchinson & Co, 1946, repr.1971)

GIBBON, Lewis, Grassic and MACDIARMID, Hugh, *Scottish Scene or The Intelligent Man's Guide to Albyn,* (Bath: Cedric Chivers, 1934, repr.1974)

GILLESPIE, Robert, *Glasgow and The Clyde,* (Robert Forrester, Glasgow, 1876)

GRIERSON, John, 'The Salt of the Earth' in Forsyth Hardy (ed), *John Grierson's Scotland,* Edinburgh: The Ramsay Head Press, 1979)

GRIEVE, Christopher, Murray, Speech at New Kilpatrick Cemetery, Bearsden at the committal service of James Barke, Author (24 March 1958) – taken from the copy in Box 10 of the Barke Papers in the Mitchell Library Glasgow

GUNN, Neil, 'Scottish Literature Class or National', *Outlook*: vol 1 no 4, July (1936), 54-58 [Part of a serial debate – see also Kerr, Lennox and Scouller, Edward]

HANNINGTON, Wal, *The Problem of the Distressed Areas,* (London: Victor Gollanz, 1937)

KERR, Lennox, 'Scottish Literature: Class or National', *Outlook*: Vol 1 No 3, June (1936), pp. 74-80 [Part of a serial debate – see also Gunn, Neill and Scouller, Edward]

KIRKWOOD, David, *My Life of Revolt,* (London: George. G. Harrap, 1935)

LINKLATER, Eric, *Magnus Merriman,* (London: Canongate, 1934, repr.1990)

LINKLATER, Eric, 'The Novel in Scotland', *Fortnightly Review*, Nov (1935) pp. 621-624

LOCHEAD, Marion, 'The Glasgow School' in *Scots Magazine* Vol 4, no 4. Jan (1926) pp. 277-81

MACDONELL, A.G. *My Scotland,* (London: 1937)

MACDIARMID, Hugh, *Albyn: Shorter Books & Monographs,* ed by Alan Riach, (Manchester: Carcanet Press Limited, 1997)

MACDIARMID, Hugh, 'A Drunk Man Looks at the Thistle', (1926)

MACLEAN, John, *In the Rapids of Revolution: Essays, Articles and Letters, 1902-23.* Edited with an introduction and commentaries by Nan Milton, (London: Allison and Busby, 1978)

MACLEHOSE, Alexander, *The Scotland of Our Sons,* (London: Alexander Maclehose & Co, 1937)

MCARTHUR, A., 'Why I wrote *No Mean City', Daily Record,* 1 Nov (1935)

MUIR, Edwin, *Scottish Journey,* (Edinburgh: Mainstream Publishing Company, 1935:1979)

MUIR, Edwin, *Scott and Scotland: The Predicament of the Scottish Writer,* (Edinburgh: Polygon Books: 1936, repr.1982)

MUIR, Edwin, *An Autobiography,* (Edinburgh: Canongate Classics, 1954, repr.1993)

MUIR, Edwin, 'Review of Scotland: That Distressed Area' by George Malcolm Thomson, in *Criterion* 15:59 Jan (1936) pp. 330-32

MUIR, James Hamilton, *Glasgow in 1901,* (William Hodge & Co, Glasgow and Edinburgh, 1901)

MUNRO, Neil, *The Clyde River and Firth,* (London: Adam & Charles Black, 1917)

MURRAY, Charles de Bois, *How Scotland is Governed,* (Edinburgh: Moray Press, 1938)

NIMLIN, Jock, 'Thoughts of an Outdoor Man', in *Weir's Way* by Tom Weir, (Edinburgh: Gordon Wright Publishing, 1981)

POWER, William, *Scotland and the Scots,* (Edinburgh: Moray Press, 1934)

POWER, William, *My Scotland,* (Edinburgh: Porpoise Press, 1934)

SCOULLER, Edward, 'Scottish Literature Class or National', *Outlook*, vol 1 no 5, August (1936), pp. 78-80 [Part of a serial debate – see also Gunn, Neill and Kerr, Lennox]

SCOULLER, Edward, 'So this is Glasgow!', *Outlook*, vol.1, no 8, November (1936), pp. 79-81

SCOULLER, Edward, 'My View of the Scots Novel', *Scotland*, vol.3, no 4, Winter (1938), pp. 49-52

SHINWELL, Emanuel, *Conflict Without Malice,* (London: Odhams Press, 1955)

SILLITOE, Percy, *Cloak Without Dagger,* (London: Cassell & Co, 1955)

SMITH, G. Gregory, *Scottish Literature: Character and Influence,* (London: Macmillan & Co, 1919, repr. 1935)

STENHOUSE, David, *Glasgow: Its Municipal Undertakings and Enterprise,* (Glasgow Corporation: Glasgow, 1933)

STEWART, Agnes, 'Some Scottish Novelists'. *The Northern Review*, vol.1, no.1, May (1924), pp. 35-41

SOUTAR, William, 'Faith in the Vernacular', in *Voice of Scotland* 1:1 June-August 1938

THOMSON, George Malcolm, *Caledonia, Or the Future of the Scots,* (London: Kegan Paul, 1927)

THOMSON, George Malcolm, *Scotland: That Distressed Area,* (Edinburgh: Porpoise Press, 1935)

Secondary sources

BELLAMY, Martin, *The Shipbuilders: An Anthology of Scottish Shipyard Life,* (Edinburgh: Birlinn, 2001)

BROOM, John, *John Maclean,* (Loanhead: MacDonald Publishers, 1973)

BURGESS, Moira, *Imagine a City: Glasgow in Fiction*, (Glendaruel: Argyll

Publishing, 1998)

BURGESS, Moira, *The Glasgow Novel,* (Glasgow: The Scottish Library Association, 2nd Edition, 1986 and 3rd Edition, 1999)

CHAPMAN, M. *The Gaelic Vision in Scottish Culture,* (London: Croom Helm, 1978)

CHECKLAND, Sydney, *The Upas Tree: Glasgow 1875-1975,* (University of Glasgow Press, 1976)

CLARK, Helen, and CARNEGIE, Elizabeth, *She was Aye Workin': Memories of Tenement Women in Edinburgh and Glasgow,* (Oxford: White Cockade, 2003)

CRAIG, David, 'The Radical Literary Tradition', ed. by Gordon Brown, *The Red Paper on Scotland,* (Edinburgh, 1975) pp. 289:303

CUNNISON, J. and GILFILLIAN, J.B.S. (eds), *Glasgow: the Third Statistical Account of Scotland,* (Glasgow: Collins, 1958)

DAMER, Seán. 'No Mean Writer? The Curious Case of Alexander McArthur', in Kevin McCarra and Hamish Whyte (eds), *A Glasgow Collection: Essays in Honour of Joe Fisher* (Glasgow City Libraries, 1990)

DAMER, Seán, *Glasgow Going for a Song,* (London: Lawrence & Wishart Ltd, 1990)

DAMER, Seán, 'Review of the Legend of Red Clydeside by Iain McLean' in *History Workshop Journal,* No 18, 1984, and McLean's reply in following edition.

DAVIES, Andrew, 'The Scottish Chicago? From hooligans to gangsters ininter-war Glasgow'. *Cultural and Social History,* Vol 4, issue 4, 2007. pp. 511-527

DEVINE, T.M. *The Tobacco Lords: A Study of the Tobacco Merchants of Glasgow and Their Trading Activities, c.1740-90,* (Edinburgh University Press, 1990)

DEVINE, T.M. *The Scottish Nation: A History 1700-2000,* (New York: Viking: 1999)

DONALDSON, William, *Popular Literature in Victorian Scotland: Language, fiction and the Press,* (Aberdeen University Press, 1986)

EAGLETON, Terry, *Marxism and Literary Criticism,* (London: Methuen, 1976)

EAGLETON, Terry, *Criticism and Ideology* (London: NLB, 1976)

EAGLETON, Terry, (ed. *Ideology* London: Longman, 1994)

EAGLETON, Terry *Literary Theory,* (Oxford: Blackwell, 1983 repr.1996)

EAGLETON, Terry and Milne, Drew, (eds) *Marxist Literary Theory* (Oxford: Blackwell, 1996)

EAGLETON, Terry, *The English Novel: An Introduction* (Oxford:Blackwell, 2005)

FINLAY, Richard, J. 'National Identity in Crisis: Politicians, Intellectuals and the "End of Scotland" 1920-1939. *History,* 79 (1994), pp.242-259

FOSTER, John, 'Scotland and the Russian Revolution' in *Scottish Labour*

History Society , 23, (1988)

FOSTER, John, 'Red Clyde, Red Scotland' in Ian Donnachie and Christopher Whatley (eds), *The Manufacture of Scottish History*, (Edinburgh: Polygon, 1992)

FRASER, W. Hamish, 'The Working Class' in Fraser and Irene Maver (eds), *Glasgow, Volume II:1830-1912*, (Manchester University Press, 1996)

FRASER, W. Hamish, 'Competing with the Capital: The Case of Glasgow Versus Edinburgh', in Lars Nilsson (ed) *Capital Cities: Images and realities in the Historical Development of European Capital Cities*, (Stockhlom University: Institute of Urban History, 2000).

GIFFORD, Douglas, *The Dear Green Place: The Novel in the West of Scotland*, (Glasgow: Third Eye Centre, 1985)

GIFFORD, Douglas, DUNNIGAN, Sarah and MACGILLIVRAY, Alan (eds) *Scottish Literature*, (Edinburgh University Press, 2002)

GLASSER, Ralph, *Growing up in the Gorbals*, (Edinburgh: Black & White Publishing, 2006)

GRAY, Alasdair, *Lanark*, (London: Palladin Books, 1981:1987)

GRAY, Alasdair, *1982 Janine*, (London: Jonathan Cape, 1984)

GRIEVE, Michael, in *Whither Scotland?* ed by D. Glen, (London: Gollancz, 1971)

HARPER, Marjory, *Emigration from Scotland Between the Wars: Opportunity or Exile*, (Manchester University Press, 1998)

HART, Francis Russell, *The Scottish Novel from Smollett to Spark*, (Cambridge Massachusetts: Harvard University Press, 1978)

HERMAN, Arthur, *The Scottish Enlightenment: The Scots Invention of the Modern World*, (London: Fourth Estate, 2002)

HORSEY, Miles, *Tenements and Towers: Glasgow Working class housing, 1890-1990*, (Royal Commission on the Ancient and Historical Monuments of Scotland, 1990)

HUTCHISON, Iain, 'Glasgow working class politics' in R. A. Cage (ed.), *The Working Class in Glasgow, 1750-1914* (Croom Helm, London, 1987)

JEFFREY, Robert, and WATSON, Ian, *Clydeside Faces and Places: The Herald Book of the Clydeside*, (Edinburgh: Black & White Publishing, 2000),

KELLETT, J.R. *Glasgow*, (Edinburgh: 1967)

KING, Elspeth, *The Hidden History of Glasgow's Women: The Thenew Factor*, (Edinburgh: Mainstream, 1993)

LINDSAY, Maurice, *Glasgow: Fabric of a City*, (London: Hale, 2001)

LUKÁCS, Georges, *History and Class Consciousness: Studies in Marxist Dialectics*, (Cambridge, Massachusetts: MIT Press, 1923, 1971)

LUKÁCS, Georges, *The Historical Novel*, (London: Merlin Press, 1937,1962)

LUKÁCS, Georges, *The Meaning of Contemporary Realism*, (London: Merlin Press,1963)

LUKÁCS, Georges, *Realism in Our Time*, (New York: Harper & Row, 1964)

LUKÁCS, Georges, *Studies in European Realism* , (New York: Grosset & Dunlap, 1964)

LUKÁCS, Georges, *The Theory of the Novel,* (London: Merlin Press, 1920)

MASSIE, Alan, *Portraits of a City,* (London: Barrie & Jenkins, 1989)

MAVER, Irene, *Glasgow*, (Edinburgh University Press, 2000)

MACDOUGALL, Ian, (ed.), *Voices from the Hunger Marches: Personal Recollections of the Scottish Hunger Marchers of the 1920s and 1930s.* Volume One and Two,(Edinburgh: Polygon, 1990, repr.1991)

MCARTHUR, C. 'The dialectic of national identity: the Glasgow Exhibition of 1938', in Bennett, T. MERCER, C. and WOOLACOTT, J. (eds), *Popular Culture and Social Relations,* (Open University Press, 1986)

MCCULLOCH, Margery Palmer, (ed.) *Modernism and Nationalism: Literature and Society in Scotland 1918 – 1939 Source documents for the Scottish Renaissance,* (Glasgow: The Association for Scottish Literary Studies, University of Glasgow, 2004)

MCKEAN, Charles, *The Scottish Thirties: An Architectural Introduction,* (Edinburgh: Royal Incorporation of Architects in Scotland, 1987)

MCKINLAY, Alan, and MORRIS, R. J. (eds), *The ILP on Clydeside, 1893-1932: from Foundation to Disintegration* (Manchester University Press, Manchester, 1991)

MCLEAN, Iain, *The Legend of Red Clydeside,* (Edinburgh: John Donald, 1983, repr.1999)

MCILVANNEY, William, *Surviving the Shipwreck*, (Edinburgh: Mainstream Publishing, 1991)

MCMANUS, Mark, and CHANDLER, Glenn, *Taggart's Glasgow,* (Oxford: Lennard Publishing, 1989)

MCMILLAN, Neil, 'Wilting or the "Poor Wee Boy Syndrome" Kelman and Masculinity', in *Edinburgh Review* No.108, p.49

MCSHANE, Harry, and SMITH, Jean, *No Mean Fighter,* (London: Pluto Press, 1978)

MITCHELL, Jack, 'The struggle for the working class novel in Scotland'. *Scottish Marxist* no 6, April (1974) pp. 40-52 no 7, October (1974) pp. 46-54; no 8 January (1975) pp. 39-48

MORGAN, Edwin, 'Who will publish Scottish poetry', *New Saltire,* No 2, Nov 1961, pp.51-56

NAIRN, Tom, 'Old and New Scottish Nationalism', in G Brown (ed), *The Red Paper On Scotland* (Edinburgh, 1975), pp47 & 49

OAKLEY, Charles, *The Second City,* (Glasgow: Blackie, 1946, repr.1976)

OSBORNE, Brian, D., QUINN, Ian, and ROBERTSON, Donald, *Glasgow's River,* (Glasgow: Lindsay Publications, 1996)

RAWLINSON, George, 'Mobilising the Unemployed: The National Unemployed Workers' Movement in the West of Scotland' in *Militant Workers: Labour and Class Conflict on the Clyde, 1900-1950. Essays in*

Honour of Harry McShane 1891-1988. Edited by Robert Duncan and Arthur McIvor. (Edinburgh: John Donald Publishers Ltd, 1992)

REID, Alastair, J. 'Red Clydesiders' (1915-1924), *Oxford Dictionary of National Biography,* (Oxford: Oxford University Press, 2004-6)

RIACH, Alan, *Representing Scotland in Literature, Popular Culture and Iconography: The Masks of the Modern Nation,* (Basingstoke: Palgrave MacMillan, 2005)

RIACH, Alan, 'The Unnatural Scene: The Fiction of Irvine Welsh' in *The Contemporary British Novel* ed James Acheson and Sarah C.E. Ross, (Edinburgh University Press, 2005)

ROBB, J.G. 'Suburb and Slum in Gorbals: Social and Residential Change 1800-1900.' in George Gordon and Brian Dicks (eds), *Scottish Urban History,* (Aberdeen University Press, 1983)

SLAVEN, Anthony, *The Development of the West of Scotland,* 1750-1960, (London: Routledge and Kegan, Paul, 1975)

SMYTH, J. J. *Labour in Glasgow, 1896-1936: Socialism, Suffrage, Sectarianism* (East Linton: Tuckwell Press, 2000)

STEGMAIER, Edmund, 'Facts and Vision in Scottish Writing of the 1920s and 1930s'. *Scottish Literary Journal,* 9 , Nov 1982, pp.67-78

SNOW, C.P., *The Realists: Portraits of Eight Novelists* (London:MacMillan, 1978)

STEWART, Stephen, 'Historians race to save pieces of the Plaza', *The Herald,* 5 July 2006

STRUTHERS, John, *About Glasgow,* (Glasgow: Struthers Advertising, 1986)

SYMONS, Jellinger, C. (1839) 'Reports from the Assistant Handloom Weavers Commissioners', cited in Fredrick Engels, *The Condition of the Working Class in England* published 1845 (London: Penguin, 1987)

WATSON, Roderick, *The Literature of Scotland.* (London: MacMillan, 1984)

WILLIAMS, Raymond, *Culture and Society.* (London: Hogarth, 1958 repr.1982)

WILLIAMS, Raymond, *Marxism and Literature,* (Oxford: Oxford University Press, 1977)

WITSCHI, Beat, *Glasgow Urban Writing and Postmodernism: A Study of Alasdair Gray's Fiction,* (Frankfurt: P. Lang, 1991)

WORSDALL, Frank, The Tenement, A Way of Life: A Social, Historical and Architectural Study of Housing in Glasgow, (Edinburgh: Chambers, 1979)

Index

L

Liberalism 8, 104
Liminality 3, 4, 9, 21, 24-25, 99, 113, 131-135
Long, H. Kingsley 1, 49

Mac

McArthur, Alexander 1, 22, 49
MacDiarmid, Hugh/ Grieve, C.M. 10, 11, 46, 59, 80, 115, 117, 119- 120, 130-132
Maclean, John 88, 92, 97, 130, 133

M

Major Operation 1, 13, 18-23, 25, 31-33, 35-36, 40, 44, 46-47, 49, 52-53, 60, 61-62, 68, 70, 80, 82-83, 87-88, 90, 92, 97-98, 101-105, 110, 114, 116, 118, 120-123, 127, 129
Masculinity 66-67, 69, 70-71, 122
Means Test 38, 45, 83-84
Modernism/modernity 12, 51, 108, 118, 120
Muir, Edwin 6, 11, 16, 31, 36, 38, 42- 44, 46, 51-52, 57-59, 61, 97-98, 115, 117, 130-131

N

Nationalism 12, 101, 131, 132, 135
Naturalism 19, 20, 119
No Mean City 1, 3, 17-19, 21-23, 25, 42, 45, 49-50, 52, 54, 55-56, 60, 63-70, 80, 89, 98, 100, 102, 106, 108- 110, 116, 121-124

P

Police 23, 63-64, 77-79, 82, 84, 87, 89-90, 93, 108, 128
Post-colonial 131
Post-industrial 1, 3, 5, 9-10, 135

QR

Realism 1, 16-20, 24-27, 71, 80, 101,
107, 113, 115-121, 123-125
Red Clydeside 1, 3, 8, 13, 21, 23-24, 41, 54, 57, 73-76, 78-79, 86, 88-89, 92, 97, 113, 121, 128-129, 133
Reification 15, 96, 131

S

Scottish Renaissance 3, 10, 11, 12, 24, 115, 130, 134
Second City 1, 3, 5, 6, 9, 21, 23-24, 27, 33, 40, 42, 47, 55, 61, 71, 83, 110, 113, 129
Second World War 1, 9-10, 28, 33-34, 44, 127
Sectarianism 4, 8, 121, 129
Shiels, Edward 1, 22, 49
Shinwell, Emanuel 76-78
Shipbuilding 5-8, 19-21, 28-31, 33-34, 36, 39, 42, 47, 91, 103, 115, 122, 125, 127, 129, 132, 135
Shipyards 21, 23-24, 29-30, 33-37, 47, 52, 60, 66, 69-70, 81, 91, 104, 127
Sillitoe, Percy 64
Social Realism 1, 18-19, 26, 113, 116, 118-121, 123
Socialism 3, 8, 73, 87, 97, 125
Strikes 8, 73-81, 86, 88, 90, 109, 128

T

The Shipbuilders 1, 13, 17-23, 25, 28-30, 32, 34-36, 42, 44-46, 49, 53, 60, 63-64, 67, 69-70, 80, 99-100, 103-104, 107, 110, 114-115, 121-124, 127
Trade unions 84, 127

UV

Violence 20, 49-50, 65, 67-68, 70, 7-79, 86, 88, 107, 110, 123-124

W

Westminster 7, 75, 89-90, 132
Women 56-58, 67, 69, 105, 121-122

Lightning Source UK Ltd.
Milton Keynes UK
UKOW040723161112

202263UK00001B/27/P